THE COLONEL'S BROTHER

by Stephanie Vale
and
a Lady

ISBN: 978-1-7373406-1-4

Many thanks to my beta readers, Cheryl, Lynn, and Tobin, for their thoughtful comments and encouragement.

More thanks to my tough but fair (and encouraging) editor, Christina Boyd. Any errors in the text are solely my own responsibility.

The cover art is adapted from a portrait of Achille Etna Michallon by Léon Coignet. Additional thanks to my cover artist, Keith Draws, for his beautiful work.

And apologies to Pat Benatar.

.

The Colonel's Brother is a variation on Jane Austen's classic novel Pride and Prejudice, and is mostly based upon characters created by Austen. The characters of Henry Fitzwilliam and his father Edward Fitzwilliam are inventions.

The story of *The Colonel's Brother* begins at the end of Chapter X of Pride and Prejudice. Elizabeth has recently learned some disturbing information from the colonel, and her anger and dislike of Darcy are at their peak.

PROLOGUE

More than once did Elizabeth, in her ramble within the park, unexpectedly meet Mr. Darcy. She felt all the perverseness of the mischance that should bring him where no one else was brought, and, to prevent its ever happening again, took care to inform him at first that it was a favourite haunt of hers. How it could occur a second time, therefore, was very odd! Yet it did, and even a third. It seemed like wilful ill-nature, or a voluntary penance, for on these occasions it was not merely a few formal inquiries and an awkward pause and then away, but he actually thought it necessary to turn back and walk with her. He never said a great deal, nor did she give herself the trouble of talking or of listening much; but it struck her in the course of their third rencontre that he was asking some odd unconnected questions—about her pleasure in being at Hunsford, her love of solitary walks, and her opinion of Mr. and Mrs. Collins's happiness; and that in speaking of Rosings and her not perfectly understanding the house, he seemed to expect that whenever she came into Kent again she would be staying _there_ too. His words seemed to imply it. Could he have Colonel Fitzwilliam in his thoughts? She supposed, if he meant anything, he must mean an allusion to what might arise in that quarter. It distressed her a little, and she was quite glad to find herself at the gate in the pales opposite the Parsonage.

She was engaged one day as she walked, in perusing Jane's last letter, and dwelling on some passages which proved that Jane had not written in spirits, when, instead of being again surprised by Mr. Darcy, she saw on looking up that Colonel Fitzwilliam was meeting her. Putting away the letter immediately and forcing a smile, she said:

"I did not know before that you ever walked this way."

"I have been making the tour of the park," he replied, "as I generally do every year, and intend to close it with a call at the

Parsonage. Are you going much farther?"

"No, I should have turned in a moment."

And accordingly she did turn, and they walked towards the Parsonage together.

"Do you certainly leave Kent on Saturday?" said she.

"Yes--if Darcy does not put it off again. But I am at his disposal. He arranges the business just as he pleases."

"And if not able to please himself in the arrangement, he has at least pleasure in the great power of choice. I do not know anybody who seems more to enjoy the power of doing what he likes than Mr. Darcy."

"He likes to have his own way very well," replied Colonel Fitzwilliam. "But so we all do. It is only that he has better means of having it than many others, because he is rich, and many others are poor. I speak feelingly. A younger son, you know, must be inured to self-denial and dependence."

"In my opinion, the younger son of an earl can know very little of either. Now seriously, what have you ever known of self-denial and dependence? When have you been prevented by want of money from going wherever you chose, or procuring anything you had a fancy for?"

"These are home questions--and perhaps I cannot say that I have experienced many hardships of that nature. But in matters of greater weight, I may suffer from want of money. Younger sons cannot marry where they like."

"Unless where they like women of fortune, which I think they very often do."

"Our habits of expense make us too dependent, and there are not many in my rank of life who can afford to marry without some attention to money."

"Is this," thought Elizabeth, "meant for me?" and she coloured at the idea; but, recovering herself, said in a lively tone, "And pray, what is the usual price of an earl's younger son? Unless the elder brother is very sickly, I suppose you would not ask above fifty thousand pounds."

He answered her in the same style, and the subject dropped. To interrupt a silence which might make him fancy her affected with what had passed, she soon afterwards said:

"I imagine your cousin brought you down with him chiefly for the sake of having someone at his disposal. I wonder he does not marry, to secure a lasting convenience of that kind. But, perhaps, his sister does as well for the present, and, as she is under his sole care, he may do what he likes with her."

"No," said Colonel Fitzwilliam, "that is an advantage which he must divide with me. I am joined with him in the guardianship of Miss Darcy."

"Are you indeed? And pray what sort of guardians do you make? Does your charge give you much trouble? Young ladies of her age are sometimes a little difficult to manage, and if she has the true Darcy spirit, she may like to have her own way."

As she spoke she observed him looking at her earnestly; and the manner in which he immediately asked her why she supposed Miss Darcy likely to give them any uneasiness, convinced her that she had somehow or other got pretty near the truth. She directly replied:

"You need not be frightened. I never heard any harm of her; and I daresay she is one of the most tractable creatures in the world. She is a very great favourite with some ladies of my acquaintance, Mrs. Hurst and Miss Bingley. I think I have heard you say that you know them."

"I know them a little. Their brother is a pleasant gentlemanlike man—he is a great friend of Darcy's."

"Oh! yes," said Elizabeth drily; "Mr. Darcy is uncommonly kind to Mr. Bingley, and takes a prodigious deal of care of him."

"Care of him! Yes, I really believe Darcy _does_ take care of him in those points where he most wants care. From something that he told me in our journey hither, I have reason to think Bingley very much indebted to him. But I ought to beg his pardon, for I have no right to suppose that Bingley was the person meant. It was all conjecture."

"What is it you mean?"

"It is a circumstance which Darcy could not wish to be generally known, because if it were to get round to the lady's family, it would be an unpleasant thing."

"You may depend upon my not mentioning it."

"And remember that I have not much reason for supposing it to be Bingley. What he told me was merely this: that he congratulated himself on having lately saved a friend from the inconveniences of a most imprudent marriage, but without mentioning names or any other particulars, and I only suspected it to be Bingley from believing him the kind of young man to get into a scrape of that sort, and from knowing them to have been together the whole of last summer."

"Did Mr. Darcy give you reasons for this interference?"

"I understood that there were some very strong objections against the lady."

"And what arts did he use to separate them?"

"He did not talk to me of his own arts," said Fitzwilliam, smiling. "He only told me what I have now told you."

Elizabeth made no answer, and walked on, her heart swelling with indignation. After watching her a little, Fitzwilliam asked her why she was so thoughtful.

"I am thinking of what you have been telling me," said she. "Your cousin's conduct does not suit my feelings. Why was he to be the judge?"

"You are rather disposed to call his interference officious?"

"I do not see what right Mr. Darcy had to decide on the propriety of his friend's inclination, or why, upon his own judgement alone, he was to determine and direct in what manner his friend was to be happy. But," she continued, recollecting herself, "as we know none of the particulars, it is not fair to condemn him. It is not to be supposed that there was much affection in the case."

"That is not an unnatural surmise," said Fitzwilliam, "but it is a lessening of the honour of my cousin's triumph very sadly."

This was spoken jestingly; but it appeared to her so just a picture of Mr. Darcy, that she would not trust herself with an answer, and therefore, abruptly changing the conversation talked on indifferent matters until they reached the Parsonage. There, shut into her own room, as soon as their visitor left them, she could think without interruption of all that she had heard. It was not to be supposed that any other people could be meant than those with whom she was connected. There could not exist in the world _two_ men over whom Mr. Darcy could have such boundless influence. That he had been concerned in the measures taken to separate Bingley and Jane she had never doubted; but she had always attributed to Miss Bingley the principal design and arrangement of them. If his own vanity, however, did not mislead him, _he_ was the cause, his pride and caprice were the cause, of all that Jane had suffered, and still continued to suffer. He had ruined for a while every hope of happiness for the most affectionate, generous heart in the world; and no one could say how lasting an evil he might have inflicted.

"There were some very strong objections against the lady," were Colonel Fitzwilliam's words; and those strong objections probably were, her having one uncle who was a country *attorney, and another who was in business in London.*

"To Jane herself," she exclaimed, "there could be no possibility of objection; all loveliness and goodness as she is!--her understanding excellent, her mind improved, and her manners captivating. Neither could anything be urged against my father, who, though with some peculiarities, has abilities Mr. Darcy himself need not disdain, and respectability which he will probably never reach." When she thought of her mother, her confidence gave way a little; but she would not allow that any objections _there_ had material weight with Mr. Darcy, whose pride, she was convinced, would receive a deeper wound from the want of importance in his friend's connections, than from their want of sense; and she was quite decided, at last, that he had been partly governed by this worst kind of pride, and partly by the wish of retaining Mr. Bingley for his sister....

Jane Austen, Pride and Prejudice, Chapter X.

Chapter 1

Perhaps ten days after Mr. Darcy and Colonel Fitzwilliam arrived in Kent, Mr. Collins returned from Rosings one morning with exciting news: an express had been delivered during his call, with the intelligence that the colonel's elder brother Henry Fitzwilliam, the Viscount Leicester and heir to the earldom, would be arriving later that evening and would stay a few days on his way to a house party in Norwich. The good parson's excitement was poorly restrained; the thrill of his anticipation of ministering to the spiritual requirements of a future Earl was almost beyond his vocabulary to describe. Yet describe it he did, at numbing length, until his wife Charlotte and cousin Elizabeth found a way to change the subject.

The gentlemen called at the parsonage the following morning. The viscount was naturally the object of much curiosity, and he did not disappoint. A youthful, vigorous, outgoing man, perhaps two inches shorter and a stone heavier than Darcy, he combined the best of his cousin's dark good looks with his brother's bright blue eyes and lively conversational gifts. After the introductions had been made and tea poured, the viscount began by engaging Mrs. Collins' younger sister Maria Lucas in an animated discussion of the fare she had enjoyed at

Rosings. Miss Lucas seemed startled that such an eminence would take an interest in her, but rising to the occasion she rendered her opinions with a vivacity seldom before seen from her. The viscount turned with laughing eyes to Elizabeth. "What say you, Miss Bennet? Is the apple tart the best thing about afternoon tea at Rosings?"

Before she could reply her cousin interceded. "Oh, no, Your Lordship, certainly the condescension of your aunt Lady Catherine is by far the best thing about afternoon tea at Rosings!"

The viscount turned toward him, his voice icy. "Pardon me, sir, I do not recall addressing a question to you." As the parson stammered and Elizabeth brought up her napkin to conceal her smile, the viscount continued. "Miss Bennet? Is it the apple tart?"

"No, sir, in my estimation it is the chocolate biscuits."

"A woman after my own heart. Yes, Lady Catherine's cook makes the best chocolate biscuits in the south of England." He put down his tea cup and moved to a chair closer to her seat. "You are from Hertfordshire, Miss Bennet? What beautiful country that is." She returned his warm smile and they began to converse in low tones, laughing softly from time to time.

Charlotte looked on with interest. It certainly seemed that the viscount admired Elizabeth, and Elizabeth seemed to be enjoying his attentions. Charlotte redoubled her social energies toward the two remaining cousins, or at least Colonel Fitzwilliam, who, whilst politely participating in the conversation with her, was looking back and forth between his brother and his cousin. Darcy, who was if possible even more quiet than usual, had taken up a position by one of the windows but seemed to be more engaged in observing the viscount and his new friend than in admiring the gardens.

After a little while the colonel stood and said, "We really must be going now, but perhaps we may call tomorrow.... Henry?"

The viscount stood. Maria blushed and curtsied deeply as he caught her eye and bowed. "How tiresome, Richard, is it already time for us to leave?"

"Yes, I am afraid so. But perhaps we may call again tomorrow or the next day."

"Very well, then. Miss Bennet, it has truly been a pleasure." He bowed over her hand. "Mrs. Collins, Mr. Collins, Miss Lucas, I have so enjoyed our visit. I hope to see you all again very soon. Darcy?"

Darcy, still standing by the window, turned around and bowed. "Yes, of course. Mr. and Mrs. Collins, Miss Lucas." His voice dropped half an octave. "Miss Bennet."

She curtsied. "Mr. Darcy. Thank you for calling."

As the cousins crossed the lane into Rosings Park, the viscount grinned. "Richard! You spoke the truth. Miss Elizabeth Bennet is uniquely charming and obviously highly intelligent."

"Aye, brother, that she is."

"Her connections are very bad," Darcy interjected. The colonel looked at him curiously.

"What do you mean, Darcy?" Henry asked. "She is obviously a gentlewoman. We spoke of her father's estate in Hertfordshire."

"Yes, her father is a gentleman, but her mother is dreadful and she has three equally dreadful sisters."

"I thought she had said that she had four sisters. Perhaps I misunderstood."

"No, her elder sister is quite genteel. It is only the mother and the younger ones who are so bad. Her mother's father was a country attorney and her uncles are in trade. Her father's estate is entailed away from the female line and she has no brothers, so the estate will be inherited by her cousin, Mr. Collins."

"Mr. Collins? The wretched parson I just met?"

"The very same."

"Darcy, you are very well informed about Miss Bennet."

Darcy cleared his throat. "My friend Bingley took a house in Hertfordshire at Michaelmas, and I joined him there to assist him in learning estate management. The neighbourhood is not large and we were all frequently thrown into company together."

The colonel observed this dialogue with increasing interest.

Henry was not a complicated, deep, bookish, or intellectual man. He was moderately clever, and had received a gentleman's education, but was in no way a scholar. He had picked up some poetry along the way as a utilitarian matter, for he had found that it was very helpful in conversations with ladies, but no studious or literary pursuit had ever made any lasting impact on his life or way of thinking. He enjoyed cards at White's and purely physical pursuits like riding, hunting, fencing, and dancing, liked to spend as much time out of doors as possible, and was devoted to his dogs. There was gossip about gaming at high stakes, but surely a future earl could afford that. There were whispers that he had trifled with a housemaid or two at Matlock, but the girls had gone quietly, well taken care of. He had reached the age of thirty without settling down but was now reconciled to searching for a bride, much to the relief of his parents Edward and Elinor Fitzwilliam, the Earl and Countess of Matlock. The colonel had not expected his brother to express quite so much interest in Miss Elizabeth, but upon reflection it was not all that surprising: Henry had complained vocally and frequently about the "dull and insipid" nature of the young ladies of the London *ton*, and declared with disgust that he would never want the mother of his future children to be such a woman. Whatever else Elizabeth Bennet might be, she was neither dull nor insipid, nor was she a woman to be trifled with.

But where Henry was a mostly open book, Darcy was harder to read. The colonel had been puzzling for a few days over Darcy's unusual behaviour, notably his willingness to call at the parsonage even though he apparently had little to say to its inhabitants, and his tendency to spend quite a lot of time looking at Miss Elizabeth during those calls and during her visits to Rosings. It was an earnest, steadfast gaze, and sometimes it appeared that it might contain admiration, but at other times it seemed nothing but absence of mind. The colonel considered Darcy's earlier harsh words about the Bennet family and decided that Darcy, always a paragon of propriety, was unlikely to have any intentions in that direction. But perhaps he might bear watching, all the same.

Chapter 2

After the visitors departed, Mr. Collins returned to his book room and Maria went to sit in the garden, leaving the friends alone together. Charlotte fixed Elizabeth with a pointed look and said nothing for several seconds. Elizabeth looked as neutral as possible and locked gazes with Charlotte for a long moment but finally erupted in laughter. "Yes, Charlotte? YES?"

"The viscount is a very handsome man."

"And charming, too, do you not agree?"

"I could not say, Lizzy, because I barely spoke with him. After he flirted with Maria he turned his attentions to you exclusively, and the rest of us got barely four words out of him until he took his leave."

Elizabeth blushed. "He expressed an interest in Hertfordshire. I enjoyed speaking with him about it."

"I am sure I heard some Wordsworth being discussed as well."

"Yes, we spoke of poetry. He is a delightful conversationalist. Perhaps not as relaxed as his brother, but certainly far superior --"

"Superior to his cousin? Is that what you were going to say, Lizzy? You know I believe Mr. Darcy admires you. It is natural for a reserved man to be reticent in the presence of a woman he admires."

"Oh, Charlotte. Please. Mr. Darcy has never shown me any sign that he has any interest in me except to criticize. I do not even think he particularly likes me."

"He has been calling here with great regularity, with and without the colonel. It must be to see you. There can be no other inducement here at the parsonage."

"Charlotte, when the alternative is being shut up at Rosings with Lady Catherine, no other inducement to escape the house can possibly be needed!"

They laughed, having resolved nothing, and spoke of other things.

That evening in the dining room at Rosings, Lady Catherine did her best to convince her newly arrived nephew to stay a few more days. "But you have just arrived, Henry! This is very disappointing. When must you go, and how is it that you need to leave us so quickly?"

"My apologies, Your Ladyship. The Duke of Norwich expects me to join him in making up a house party at Featherdale. But I shall remain there for only a fortnight, and as my brother and cousin Darcy shall remain here, I shall be glad to return to Rosings on my way back to London."

"It is hardly 'on your way,'" intoned Darcy, so faintly that the colonel, seated at his right, was not quite certain he had heard him, but absolutely certain that the viscount had not, nor had he been intended to.

"Very well, then," Lady Catherine grumbled. "Do as you must. We shall all be happy to greet you upon your return."

"Some more than others," Darcy muttered, again heard only by the colonel.

***

The Viscount Leicester was to depart only two days hence, and on the following day the three young men once again strolled to the parsonage. It was a glorious spring day, cool and sunny, and the viscount was in a jovial, exuberant mood. As the colonel teased his brother for having won the heart of young Maria Lucas with his spirited discussion of puddings, he noticed that his cousin was silent, his jaw set, his brow creased into a slight frown.

"Darcy! It is a beautiful day, and we are about to call upon a beautiful woman. Surely you can muster a smile over that." The viscount laughed and walked faster. He was a few paces ahead of the others before Darcy replied.

"Excuse me? Oh, yes, yes. I am sorry. I was woolgathering.... Mrs. Collins is a very pleasant woman but I am not sure I would call her beautiful."

"You know perfectly well I was not speaking of Mrs. Collins, but let us speak of her now. Would you say she is … tolerable, but not handsome enough to tempt you?" The colonel looked at his cousin expectantly.

"Where did you –? Who told you –? Miss Elizabeth told you? She heard me?" Darcy's face was a mask of horror.

"She heard you. She told me about it herself. She was laughing when she told me but she more or less acknowledged that she did not consider it humourous at the time, in fact that you offended her and most of her neighbours. As she tells it, the story was circulated widely in the neighbourhood within a day or two of the incident."

"I must explain how this happened. It had been but a few weeks after Ramsgate, and I was still in a foul humour. Bingley forced me to attend a local assembly shortly after I arrived at his house in Hertfordshire."

The colonel was skeptical. "He forced you, Cousin? Charles Bingley, son of a tradesman, forced Fitzwilliam Darcy, master of Pemberley, to attend an assembly?"

"Yes, I will say that he forced me, for if I had refused to go, I would have had to remain at home and spend the evening with his sisters, and there are very few fates I should not choose before that."

Colonel Fitzwilliam chuckled. He had met the Bingley sisters.

"I was in a considerable ill-humour and not inclined to dance. As you know, I am seldom so inclined. In any event, Bingley decided to fall in love with a very handsome local girl and danced with her several times. He came to me to urge me to dance with her sister and I rebuffed him with those words."

"Wait, Bingley's lady-love is Miss Elizabeth's sister? One

of the dreadful ones?"

"No, her elder sister Jane, a very genteel and handsome girl."

"In any event, you insulted Miss Elizabeth in those words within her hearing. No wonder she—"

"No wonder she what? I did not intend her to hear me! Do you think me so completely witless and lacking in good manners as that?"

"Well, she did hear you, Cousin, and although she herself is far too polite to say much, I think it is clear that you are not in her good books." *I wish I had not told her about the good care Darcy takes of his friend Bingley. He will not be happy that she also knows about his efforts to part Bingley from her sister.*

"I must apologise. It is the only thing to do."

"I fear we need to have another conversation before you do that, Cousin."

Darcy stood still for a moment, pondering. By now the viscount was far ahead on the path to the parsonage and the colonel was scrambling after him. Darcy followed and in a few moments the three were received, apologetically, by Mrs. Collins and her sister. It seemed Miss Elizabeth had not yet returned from her morning walk.

As the visitors sipped their tea, they did their best to convince the sceptical Mrs. Collins that they were perfectly content with her company by energetically making conversation without repeatedly asking how long ago Miss Elizabeth had left, and how soon she might be expected back.

Darcy took up his usual position by a window. After a few minutes Elizabeth strode into view, skipping down the path from the park, her bonnet off, her face turned joyfully to the sun, a vision of health, vigor, and contentment. His lips turned up at the corners in a smile he would not have been eager to explain to his cousins.

As he gazed at her he felt almost as if he were invading her privacy, but dismissed that thought as silly since she was out of doors, after all. He took a half step back from the window against the possibility that she might look up at the house, adopted a neutral expression, and returned to the group. Shortly Elizabeth's voice could be heard in the hallway, speaking with the housemaid, before she entered the room. Her cheeks and eyes were just as bright as they had been on that autumn morning an age ago when she had burst into the breakfast room at Netherfield after walking three miles from her home at Longbourn to see to her sister, and although her hair, apparel, and especially her shoes were in somewhat better order today than they had been on that morning, Darcy felt that a certain amount of dishevelment suited her very well indeed.

How much dishevelment, and exactly how well it suited her, he resolved not to dwell upon.

The gentlemen all expressed their pleasure in being able to see her. As Darcy had feared, the viscount had somehow maneuvered himself into a position that enabled him to join Elizabeth on one of the settees. Darcy contented himself with reflecting that Henry was, after all, leaving tomorrow for two weeks, and that the sensible Miss Elizabeth was unlikely to fall in love with Henry during a morning call.

Or could she? Henry and Elizabeth were already laughing together, something about music and Lady Catherine. Darcy could just make out the words "great proficient" before hearing more peals of laughter. He cleared his throat and suddenly everyone was looking at him. *I had better say something,* he thought. He cleared his throat again. "Henry, kindly tell us about the house party you are going to tomorrow."

"Yes, Your Lordship," Elizabeth agreed. "Please tell us all about the house party."

"At Cambridge I became friendly with James Dunmore, then the heir of the Duke of Norwich. His family seat is Featherdale, near the sea at Sheringham, and I visited him there several times." He glanced over at his brother. "Richard is well acquainted with his brother Thomas, who was in the Army and is now a barrister in London."

"Yes!" The colonel smiled widely. "I have known Thomas for some years. He is a very good man. He was injured in battle and was unable to return to active service."

Henry resumed his account. "James' and Thomas' parents were killed in a carriage accident four years ago and James succeeded to the title but fell into a prolonged period of melancholy and mourning. Finally, the year before last, he returned to town for the Season and perhaps a year later married. He seems quite happy in the married state, and recommends it to all his friends with great enthusiasm," he added, glancing down at Elizabeth in a way that made her blush and look away.

Darcy's jaw clenched. Only the colonel noticed.

"Happily, since then he has resumed many of the social activities that are customary for a gentleman of his station. He is now resolved to host his first house party and has asked a few of his oldest friends to join him for the fortnight. Of course I agreed. We will ride and shoot and play cards and perhaps even do a little sea-bathing. James – His Lordship – has also advised me that he intends to give a ball while we are there. I dearly love to dance and I am looking forward to the ball."

"That is a fine plan, Your Lordship," said Elizabeth. "No wonder you are so eager to visit your friend."

"I find I am less eager to leave Rosings than I expected to be," he replied, gazing into her eyes, "and I am glad to remember that I will return here in only a fortnight. I have found Rosings far more ... congenial ... on this visit than I have ever found it in the past." Catching himself, he looked up at his brother, who was studying him. "Do you not agree, Richard, that Rosings is uncommonly improved this year?"

Richard nodded. "Darcy" — he touched his cousin's shoulder to attract his attention— "and I can certainly say that we have found more enjoyment on this visit than we have in the past. Is that not so, Darcy?" He *would* make his taciturn cousin stop staring at Miss Elizabeth and speak.

Darcy, attention recalled from his private reflections, was quick to reply. "I could not agree more, Cousin. We are grateful to you, Mrs. Collins — and your guests, of course" — nodding at Elizabeth — for offering us such a pleasant alternative to our usual occupations at Rosings."

"And now," Richard added, "it is time for us to be going.

We have trespassed on your kind hospitality long enough, Mrs. Collins. But I am sure that Darcy and I would like to call again soon, perhaps even tomorrow." He looked expectantly at Darcy, who stepped up smartly to his cousin's unspoken expectations.

"Yes, it will be our pleasure." Darcy's bow was all that was correct to his hostess, her sister, and friend. Henry, meanwhile, had possessed himself of Elizabeth's hand and was bowing over it ceremoniously. "Miss Bennet! I shall see you in a fortnight. You will still be here then, will you not?"

"I believe so, Your Lordship. Miss Lucas and I expect to be here for another three weeks at least."

"Until we meet again, then."

She curtsied and nodded. Charlotte and Maria curtsied, and the gentlemen took their leave.

***

Colonel Fitzwilliam's mind was reeling as he led his brother and cousin away from the parsonage. He was a veteran of many a successful military campaign, but the challenge he contemplated for himself this time was fearsome indeed. First, to convince his proper cousin that a dowerless country gentlewoman whom he could love – nay, already loved, it seemed – and who could make him laugh was a better choice for matrimony than any of the wealthy and proper young ladies of the London *ton*. Second, to convince Miss Elizabeth that the man who had rudely scorned her at the Meryton assembly a few months ago, and then ruined her sister's happiness, was capable of admitting that he had been wrong, making amends, courting her properly, and showing her enough of his fundamental goodness that he could win her heart.

He had a fortnight. Better call it just thirteen days. All must be resolved before Henry returned to the scene.

Chapter 3

It is said that an army travels on its stomach, and true to adage Colonel Fitzwilliam launched Day 1 of his thirteen-day campaign at Lady Catherine's breakfast table early the next morning. He knew Darcy would also be up early, and thought it likely that Anne and her mother would not stir for another hour or two at least, allowing the privacy they required. He sipped a cup of coffee and turned over the plan in his mind. It was incomplete and contained far too many loose ends, but it was the best he could do.

As he tucked into a plate of ham and eggs, his unsuspecting cousin strolled into the breakfast parlour, poured himself some coffee, and investigated the various fragrant chafing dishes. "Good morning, Richard. Has Henry departed already?"

"Good morning. Yes, he was off half an hour ago."

"It has been strange, having him here. I am so accustomed to making these visits with you alone."

"Yes, I know what you mean. My brother can be ... distracting company."

Darcy looked up from his plate. "Distracting? Yes, that is a good word for it. Distracting."

"Well, now that the distraction is gone for a fortnight, I hope you will be able to take advantage."

"Take advantage? I do not understand."

Colonel Fitzwilliam sighed. *My stubborn cousin is going to make this harder than it needs to be.*

"I am speaking of Miss Elizabeth."

"I would never try to take advantage of Miss Elizabeth! What do you take me for?"

"Be quiet for a minute. We spoke of your desire, your need to apologise to Miss Elizabeth. Today is the day! Without Henry distracting her, you will have her undivided attention."

"I am beginning to doubt that I can do it. I cannot possibly speak of those things in front of Mrs. Collins or her sister, or worse yet Mrs. Collins' odious toad of a husband. And I cannot ask for a private interview. That would raise questions. Expectations."

"Darcy, did my dear aunt Anne drop you on your head when you were a baby?"

"Pardon?"

"Never mind. What does Miss Elizabeth like to do in the mornings?" Darcy looked at him blankly. *Could he really be that obtuse?* "Why was she not in when we arrived yesterday?"

He saw the light come into Darcy's eyes. "She walks in the park. In the grove."

"Precisely. You need only happen to encounter her while out walking yourself. It is perfectly proper. You can speak privately because you are out of doors, and you can walk as long and as far as you need to in order to say your piece."

"Richard, you are a genius. You will be a general someday." Darcy took a final sip of coffee, dabbed his lips with his linen napkin, and stood up. "It is a beautiful morning, and I am in sore need of a walk before I take up Rosings' ledgers again today."

"Before you go, Darcy, one more thing. You recall I mentioned yesterday that we needed to have another conversation before you embarked on your apology?"

"Yes?"

"You will actually need to make two apologies."

"Two? What else have I done?"

"Miss Elizabeth knows that you were responsible for Charles Bingley leaving Hertfordshire so abruptly."

Darcy dropped back into his chair. "How could she know that?"

"Because I told her."

"You *what*? What exactly did you say to her, and why on earth would you tell her such a thing?"

"Calm down, Cousin, I thought I was paying a compliment to you about your willingness to look out for a friend. I had no idea the lady involved was Miss Elizabeth's sister! But she was obviously disturbed by our discussion. She criticized your actions as officious. She asked how you could possibly be so confident that it was proper to effect Mr. Bingley's separation from a lady he cared for, and who loved him. I thought her reaction was purely theoretical until yesterday when you told me that the lady Bingley loved was her sister."

"Wait, she said a lady he cared for, *and who loved him?*"

"Yes, now that you mention it, I wondered why she leapt to that assumption. But she knew. You said this sister was genteel, Darcy. Was the family really that bad? It is hard to imagine a woman like Miss Elizabeth coming from—"

"Yes, Richard, they are that bad, particularly the mother and younger sisters. You must trust me on this."

"And yet *you* ..." Richard paused, looking for the right words.

"And yet I what?"

"Darcy, I have never seen you so affected by a woman as you are by Elizabeth Bennet. You look at her constantly and attend to her every syllable. It is obvious that Henry's ease in conversation with her, his casual flirtation with her, has been distressing you. I think you are in love with her."

Darcy was silent. He opened his mouth as if to speak and then closed it again, shaking his head.

"Yes, Cousin, I believe you are in love. And why should you not be? She is charming, beautiful, and intelligent. She is a gentlewoman no matter how bad some of her family may be. Do not forget, Darcy, you are related to Aunt Catherine! Can any of the Bennets' family members be that bad?" The colonel looked at him sympathetically.

After a moment Darcy found his voice. "And supposing that I *were* in love with her, what of it? Henry can make her a viscountess, then a countess."

"Do you really believe that she cares about that?"

"Her mother would."

"Darcy, based upon your own account of the family, I have the distinct impression that Miss Elizabeth is not heavily influenced by her mother."

Darcy chuckled. "Nay, that she is not."

"So what is the difficulty?"

"Well, Cousin, based upon the information I have recently received from you, it appears that she may have two excellent reasons to despise me."

"Even if she does have two reasons to despise you, or more likely, to be angry with you, you have two weeks to apologise, to convince her of your sincere regrets, to make amends. You have two whole weeks, without Henry distracting her, to make her see that as a matter of substance over style, you are the man who deserves to win her."

"Your brother will not appreciate your coaching and

intervention on my behalf."

"My brother will never know. He is oblivious to your interest. When he left this morning he did not say a word about forwarding his suit with Miss Elizabeth or keeping you away from her in his absence. I doubt he will give her a moment's thought while he is at Featherdale, and if you were to ask him, he would tell you he believes that his title and flirtatious words will keep her on the string until he returns and decides whether to reel her in. In a fortnight when he returns and you are engaged to Miss Elizabeth—"

"You are getting ahead of yourself, Richard."

"In a fortnight when Henry returns and *you are engaged to Miss Elizabeth*, he will congratulate both of you and move on to find a woman who likes riding and cards more than books and music. I do not believe that Henry and Miss Elizabeth would suit at all. But she would be so good for you, Darcy. And you for her. You must win her over."

Darcy mulled the colonel's words. There was no point in arguing with his cousin, especially as he had long since lost the same argument with himself. He looked up with hope in his eyes. "She is remarkable, is she not?"

"I will say it again. She is beautiful, charming, intelligent. She is clever, witty, kind, and every good thing. She is different from the ladies you have met in London, Darcy. There is an authenticity about her that is very appealing. This is why I say that you must win her over. Your fortune will not be sufficient inducement for Miss Elizabeth, just as my brother's title is not. You must open your heart and let her see the good, honourable, generous, caring man you are, moreover a man who loves her. I doubt she will be able to resist that man. But she has not really met him yet."

"You are quite the matchmaker, Richard."

"Darcy, I have been in the army for twelve years now. I have had to become more observant, to learn how to size men up on short notice, what motivates them, how to see into their souls to predict how they will perform on the battlefield. This is not so different."

"Love is a battlefield?"

"The marriage mart is a battlefield, let us put it that way. You have before you the prospect of a love match. Go out and make it happen."

"Aunt Catherine will—"

"Put her out of your mind. Focus on the job at hand. There is enough time to worry about Aunt Catherine's reaction when you are flush with the joy of winning your lady's hand. Your happiness will give you all the strength you need then. But first you have to get there, Darcy. The doubts will kill your initiative if you allow them."

"You really think—"

"I really think that you and Miss Elizabeth would suit each other in every possible way. She would be so good for you, Cousin. And you would be good for her. You already love her. Now, let her get to know you, the true you, so that she can reciprocate your feelings."

Darcy rose again, less forcefully this time. "Then I need to go for a walk now."

"Yes, you do. Do not allow me to delay you." The colonel inclined his head. "You will find me in Lady Catherine's book room when you return. And Darcy—"

"Yes, Richard?"

"Do not botch this."

Darcy laughed shortly and turned to exit the breakfast parlour. "Anne! Good morning!" He wondered how long she had been standing by the door.

Chapter 4

Darcy had been in the park for almost a quarter hour before he glimpsed a flash of something that might have been blue muslin and began to walk in that direction. A few minutes later he was rewarded with the "accidental" encounter he had been hoping for. "Miss Elizabeth!"

"Mr. Darcy." Her voice was cool but her curtsey was correct. He bowed in the same degree.

"I am glad to see you. I have been hoping for an opportunity to speak with you, Miss Elizabeth. Would you do me the honour of walking with me for a few minutes?"

In those beautiful eyes he thought he saw a flicker of distrust and anger, but when she looked back up at him her countenance betrayed no emotion. "Very well, sir."

He extended his arm and after a long moment she took it. The brim of her bonnet obscured his view of her face. He wondered idly whether that would make his task easier or harder. Surely it was hard enough already. *Time to begin. Take a deep breath.*

"Miss Elizabeth, I believe I owe you an apology and an explanation, and possibly a second apology."

She had had no idea what to expect, but this was not it. They were both silent for a few moments.

"You may be certain that you have my full attention, sir."

Dash it, I was hoping that once I began it would become easier. "My first apology is for some graceless words I uttered at the assembly in Meryton the night you and I first met."

She stopped walking and turned to face him. "As I recall, we were not actually introduced on that occasion, but pray continue, Mr. Darcy."

"I insulted you abominably. I called you tolerable, but not handsome enough to tempt me."

"So you did."

"Miss Elizabeth, I have no excuse, but I should like to explain."

"Go on, please." She was looking directly at him. This was a hopeful sign, he felt. He looked into those fine dark eyes and forged ahead.

"I had recently experienced a very distressing event involving a family member, something Colonel Fitzwilliam is aware of but Lady Catherine, Anne, and the viscount are not. I cannot say more at this moment except to tell you that it was horrible in every way. I was in a foul humour for weeks and during that time Bingley asked me to come to Hertfordshire and help him set up his new country house and learn his estate responsibilities. I agreed to do so, against my inclination, because Bingley is one of my dearest friends. When I arrived, I learned that he had undertaken for me to attend the local assembly with him the very next evening. I had no interest in trying to engage in social niceties with strangers, since as you know it is not my talent, and as you also know, dancing is something I am rarely inclined to do. But I agreed to attend the event with him, feeling that in so doing I had fully honoured his undertaking. And then once we were there Bingley tried to persuade me to dance, and that was when I lashed out at him. I was willing to say almost anything to make him leave me be."

"And so you did." She broke their gaze and looked down at the ground.

"Yes." He took a deep breath. "Miss Elizabeth, please understand. I am not merely apologising for the rudeness of the words or for the fact that you overheard. Beyond the rudeness, and beyond your becoming aware of the rudeness, I want you to understand that I am sorry on my own account that I ever formed those words. I do not consider them accurate, and even at the time they did not represent my true opinion. I do not even know where they came from. I beg you to accept my most sincere and heartfelt apology." He paused and took a deep breath.

She continued to look down at the ground. She had rather enjoyed holding this grudge against him. It made things simpler. But if he truly didn't consider her merely tolerable, could Charlotte be correct? No, that was impossible. In any event, he was waiting for her to respond. She felt moisture in her eyes, and blinked a few times before looking back up at him. His dark brown eyes were full of emotion, an emotion she did not recognise. She could not look away again. "I thank you for that, Mr. Darcy. It could not have been easy for you. I accept your apology." The next emotion she saw in his eyes was one she did recognise: relief. She reached out involuntarily and touched his gloved hand. "Truly."

"Thank you, Miss Elizabeth."

She grinned. "I must now ask you, Mr. Darcy, whether this means I may assume that in your eyes my appearance is better than tolerable."

She is teasing me! This is good. "Miss Elizabeth, it can certainly not be proper for me to respond to that question."

She laughed. "Fair enough, sir."

"And now that we have agreed that it is not proper for me to do so, I will tell you that, yes, I consider you far more than tolerable."

She looked down at the ground again. When she looked up her cheeks were pink and she was smiling. "Then I thank you for the lovely but improper compliment, sir."

"And you are very welcome." He took a long breath and exhaled. *This is so pleasant. Must I really start in on the other thing right away?* He allowed a few seconds to pass. Blessed silence and perhaps, if he was lucky, the beginning of an amicable understanding.

"Mr. Darcy, I do not wish to be impolite, but I believe it is time for me to return to the parsonage. I have been out walking for quite a while and Mrs. Collins will wonder what has become of me. You said you had another matter to discuss with me. Would it be possible for us to have that discussion at another time?"

Oh, yes, yes, yes. "Yes, certainly, Miss Elizabeth, I do not wish to detain you against your will. But I do wish to speak with you again soon. Will you walk out tomorrow morning?"

"Weather permitting, I walk out every morning. Perhaps I will see you tomorrow then?"

"You may rely upon it."

"Very well then." She extended her hand, voluntarily this time, and he bowed over it, pressing it perhaps a moment longer than necessary. She curtsied and was gone.

Chapter 5

Darcy sat down on a nearby stump to collect his thoughts and consider his morning's efforts. *She accepted my apology. Can I be certain she was sincere? She seemed sincere. I have never known her to dissemble in any way. And she teased me about it! She truly did accept it. This is progress. Richard will be pleased. I am pleased. I am ... encouraged. A little.*

Elizabeth's thoughts were more confused as she hurried back to the parsonage. *What is he about? Two apologies and an explanation? Why has the proud Mr. Darcy decided to apologise and explain himself to me? What on earth can he have to say to me tomorrow?*

Her agitation was such that after accepting a cup of tea from Charlotte she pled a headache and retired to her room to lie down, although the disquiet of her mind kept rest at bay.

Darcy headed back to Rosings with a lighter heart than he had enjoyed in weeks. Even his aunt's greeting upon his return to the house could not dampen his mood. "Nephew! There you are! I asked Richard and he said you had gone for a walk? This is not your usual habit. Is all well with you?"

"Yes, Aunt. It was a beautiful morning and so I decided that a walk in your Ladyship's park would be a good way to start the day after breakfast."

"Very well. If tomorrow is an equally pleasant day, you should take Anne out for a drive in her phaeton. It would be pleasant for both of you and it would give you more opportunity to spend time together."

"Perhaps so," he replied, not knowing what else to say. "And now, Aunt, I am for the book room and reviewing the ledgers." He moved swiftly down the hall and got the book room door safely closed behind him before she could say anything else. *Peace.*

"Darcy! How was your walk?"

No peace. At least not yet. "It was ... good, Richard. We did not have time to get through everything that needed to be said. I did apologise for my words at the assembly in Hertfordshire."

"And she accepted the apology?"

"Yes, I believe so. She said she did, and she teased me about it afterwards, so I believe she was sincere."

"She teased you? Excellent. Do you want to tell me more about it?"

"No, truly, I do not. I do hope that by this time tomorrow we will be through the second apology and at least the air between us will be cleared."

"Shall we call on the parsonage later today? Would it be

awkward?"

"Possibly, but Mrs. Collins might be expecting us, so perhaps we should go for at least a few minutes. Let us walk over to the parsonage in the afternoon."

It is safe to say that very little useful work was accomplished in the book room in the next few hours.

At the midday meal Anne, her companion Mrs. Jenkinson, and Lady Catherine joined Darcy and Fitzwilliam in the dining room. Over vegetable soup and capons Her Ladyship vented her displeasure over the cost of renovations to her stables, which were not in good repair due to her neglect of their upkeep despite years of reminders from her nephews. Finally, Darcy had consulted with Anne and then given direction that improvements were to be made, that a certain amount of money was allocated to be spent, and that no change in direction or instruction from Lady Catherine was to be honored unless he or Anne confirmed its validity. Her Ladyship was quite put out, but Darcy endured her harangue with a bland patience Colonel Fitzwilliam and Anne found marvelous. Seated across from one another, the two shared amused glances every time Darcy responded "Yes, Aunt Catherine," or "No, Aunt Catherine," or "That is correct, Aunt Catherine," or occasionally, "That is not correct, Aunt Catherine," or another mild and polite rejoinder to one of her ladyship's provocations.

"It is my money, after all, and my stables."

"Yes, Aunt Catherine."

"This roof you are putting up! It will cost almost three

hundred pounds."

"That is correct, Aunt Catherine."

"Those workers are thieves. A stable roof cannot possibly cost three hundred pounds."

Fitzwilliam was tempted to remind her about the cost of her chimneypiece but held his tongue, as Darcy responded with the same mildness he had been exhibiting for the last half hour. "That is not correct, Aunt Catherine. I have maintained the stable roofs at Pemberley to a very high standard, but even so, when a partial replacement was needed for one of them last year the cost was more than two hundred pounds. These things can be expensive, but they must be done to preserve the value and the good name of Rosings."

Darcy knew that bringing the subject back around to Rosings and its value was the way to win this argument with his aunt, even though a moment of awkwardness was guaranteed to follow.

"Yes, Rosings! When you and Anne are married I hope you will still choose to spend time here, and then your second son can have it."

Darcy glanced at his cousin Anne, reflexively, and she at him. She gave him a tiny smile. They had discussed this problem many times and neither of them had any wish to wed the other. Anne's health was not vigorous and she certainly did not wish to bear any man heirs, even if the second son could grow up to inherit Rosings. Anne was already the owner of Rosings; under the terms of her father's will she had come into possession on her twenty-fifth birthday, and she took comfort from knowing that should her mother ever become wholly intolerable, she could pack her off to the dower house. Still, "wholly intolerable," like other descriptions, must be in the eye of the beholder, and Anne's tolerance for her mother far exceeded that of most of their relations.

Darcy waited until Lady Catherine began speaking again and shot Anne a quick wink in return, then looked down before his aunt could notice. He was grateful for Anne's support. It was not yet quite necessary to tell Lady Catherine explicitly that he and Anne could never be married, but he devoutly hoped that the appropriate moment would come very soon, specifically within the next twelve days.

When he looked up the footman, Harrison, had come in with a plate of chocolate biscuits. He took one and watched as Richard whispered something to Harrison. He was not the only person at the table who noticed this.

"What is it, Richard? What are you saying to Harrison? I must have my part in the conversation."

"Yes, Aunt Catherine. A few days ago at the parsonage there was a discussion about the excellence of the chocolate biscuits at Rosings. I was asking Harrison to ask Cook if we could have a few biscuits to take to Mrs. Collins and her guests."

"So Mrs. Collins likes my chocolate biscuits, does she?"

"Even Henry was remarking that your cook makes the best chocolate biscuits in the south of England."

"Dear Henry! He has loved those biscuits since he was a child. Yes, by all means, Richard, take a few biscuits over to the parsonage, but do not let Mr. Collins eat more than one. He is already far too fat for a man of his age. He does not look in health. I cannot be expected to replace my parson twice in two years."

"I will do my best, Aunt."

Harrison reappeared with a small parcel wrapped in paper and tied with string. "Excellent, Harrison, thank you very much! Aunt Catherine, if we may.... Darcy, shall we?" Both men stood to leave.

"You are very eager to visit the parsonage, Richard. Have you developed a *tendre* for Miss Bennet?"

Darcy coughed and Richard looked startled. "Aunt Catherine. Please. Mrs. Collins and her sister and her friend are all charming ladies it is a pleasure to visit."

"That was not my question, Richard."

"I do like Miss Bennet, Aunt Catherine, but not in any extraordinary way."

"Her connections are very bad, you know."

Darcy winced at his imperious aunt's use of the very same words he had spoken a few days before.

"And she has no money."

"Do not concern yourself, Aunt Catherine. I know my situation very well. I mean only to deliver some delicious biscuits to three charming ladies."

"Very well then, be off with you."

Dismissed from the table, the cousins made haste to the front door, claimed their hats and walking sticks, and set out toward the parsonage. By tacit agreement they did not speak until they were safely away from the great house, then both began at once.

"Richard -- "

"Darcy – never mind, go ahead."

"Good heavens, Richard, did I sound like Lady Catherine a few days ago when I spoke of Miss Elizabeth's connections? How dreadful."

"Do you want the truth? Yes."

"Is that what I have become?"

"No, you were on the brink, but you have saved yourself, or rather, Miss Elizabeth has saved you."

"She has not saved me yet."

"Yes, she has. Simply by acknowledging that you love her, and by apologizing to her for your past bad behaviour, you are saved. You will never speak that way of anyone again, because your eyes have been opened. Mine were opened when I went into the army, and met so many fine, courageous, truly noble men who would not have been received in any drawing room in the *ton*. Your eyes were opened in a different way, that is all."

Darcy reflected on his cousin's words. "Thank you, Richard. I know I have some difficult times ahead with her, but now that I have accepted and acknowledged my feelings I am more at peace than I have been in months."

"Months? You have been fighting this for months? How long have you loved her?"

"I do not know exactly, but she has exerted a kind of fascination over me almost since the moment I first saw her. I cannot say when exactly that fascination developed into a deeper feeling. I was in the middle before I knew I had begun. Having Caroline Bingley as an ever-present Greek chorus did not make it easier." He chuckled dryly.

"Miss Bingley has not given up on you, has she?"

"It appears not. Her brother apologises to me constantly. I avoid her as much as possible because I do not think it beneath her to manoeuvre an apparent compromise. At Bingley's own suggestion I locked both my bedchamber and dressing room doors every night when I slept at Netherfield."

"Surely you do not think – surely he does not think..."

"I have no way of knowing. But I am not interested in learning the hard way."

"Let us speak of happier things. Here we are at the parsonage, with a parcel of chocolate biscuits!"

But the parsonage inhabitants were out, so they left the parcel with instructions to give it to Miss Elizabeth, and returned to the great house and to their labours in the book room. The colonel sensed that his taciturn cousin had bled freely during their earlier discussions and took pity on him; they discussed only the ledgers and other neutral subjects for the rest of the day.

Chapter 6

At breakfast on Day 2 Darcy and the colonel chatted amiably about everything except that which was uppermost in both their minds. Perhaps Darcy lingered an extra minute or two over his coffee, and there were moments when it seemed he might have something meaningful to say, but his cousin never forced the issue. Finally Darcy stood. "I believe I fancy an early walk before I begin to work, Richard."

Richard only smiled. "And I need to get back to the book room. I will see you there later. I hope you have a good walk."

Darcy nodded and was gone. Richard took another scone, smeared it with jam, and muttered, "Good luck, Cousin."

"Good luck in what?" Anne had entered the breakfast parlour undetected again. "Richard, will you please talk to me about what is going on with you and Darcy?"

This was a complication, yet potentially a good one. He nodded. "Yes, but I think not here. Will you meet me in the book room after your breakfast? We will not be disturbed there."

"That will do nicely." Once her mother came down there could be no conversation that excluded Her Ladyship. "I will see you there."

Forty minutes later found Anne entering the library. Colonel Fitzwilliam was seated at the desk bent over a large leatherbound ledger but looked up when she came in. "Sit down, Cousin. Shall I ring for tea or coffee?"

"No, thank you, Richard, I just came from breakfast."

"Of course."

Neither spoke for a moment. Finally Anne decided the initiative was hers to take. "Richard, what is going on with Darcy? Does it have something to do with Henry? He seemed almost indecently glad to see Henry take his leave. Have they quarreled? Why were you wishing him good luck today?.... Wait, does this have anything to do with Miss Elizabeth?"

Richard grinned. "You have cut to the heart of it, Annie."

"To the heart of what? I am still confused."

"When Henry was here he was very taken with Miss Elizabeth."

"I heard Mother saying something that made me wonder if that was happening. And why should he not be taken with her? She is charming, genteel, intelligent, and very beautiful."

"So she is. It happens that Henry spent a lot of time monopolizing her attention, making her laugh, speaking of poetry, you know, all the things Henry does when he likes a pretty girl."

"Do you think she returns his interest?"

"It is obvious that she was flattered to be the object of his attentions. But the situation is more complex than that. Darcy is in love with her."

"Darcy is in love with Miss Elizabeth?" *Mother cannot be allowed to find this out.*

"Yes. Although it was difficult to induce him to admit it, I have never seen a woman affect him this way. It was an agony for him to sit by and watch Henry flirting with her, making her laugh, always taking the seat next to her, and so forth."

"No wonder he was so glad to see Henry go. He is using this fortnight of Henry's absence to court Miss Elizabeth? That is why you were wishing him luck?"

"In a manner of speaking, yes. But he has some amends to make with her before he can begin to even hope to court her. Thirty-six hours ago he owed her two important apologies. Yesterday morning he succeeded in making the first one –"

"Two apologies? Darcy?! His manners are impeccable."

"Usually. The first was a real lapse for Darcy. The details are not important, but he insulted Miss Elizabeth's appearance at an assembly in Hertfordshire, and she overheard him."

"Good heavens."

"I know; it gets worse. That was only the first apology. The second will be far more difficult. Do you know Darcy's friend Bingley?"

"We have not met, but I hear that he is a very amiable, gentlemanlike man."

"Exactly. Well, the whole reason Darcy was in Hertfordshire with Bingley in the autumn was to assist Bingley in taking over the management of an estate he had leased. While they were in the neighbourhood Bingley fell in love with Miss Elizabeth's elder sister Jane, who by all accounts is a delightful young woman and became very attached to Bingley in turn."

"That sounds like happy news."

"It would be if Darcy had not persuaded Bingley that Miss Jane Bennet did not love him, and that he should leave Hertfordshire and never come back."

"He did *what*?"

"You heard me."

"Darcy did this? Why? What possessed him? How painful for Bingley, and how awful for Miss Jane Bennet."

"Yes, I gather it has been dreadful for them both, and Darcy has no really satisfactory explanation for his actions. It seems that Miss Jane Bennet is all that is proper and reserved, and Darcy doubted her attachment to his friend. Darcy says he only wished to spare his friend a marriage without affection."

"I still do not understand. It was a dreadful thing to do, certainly, but how could Miss Elizabeth have found out about it?"

Richard hesitated. "I told her."

"You told her? Why would you—?"

"Yes, I told her. Do not look at me that way, Cousin. I did not realise when I told her the story that I was speaking of her sister! I knew that Miss Elizabeth was not favourably disposed toward Darcy and I wished her to know about the prodigiously good care he takes of his friends, and before I knew it I was giving her examples, including his recently saving one of his closest friends from an imprudent marriage."

"You said 'imprudent marriage?'"

"I said worse. I believe I uttered the words, 'there were some very strong objections against the lady.' Mind you, I heard that explanation first from Darcy."

"Oh, Richard."

"So today it was Darcy's mission to meet Miss Elizabeth during her morning walk in the grove and apologise for his officious interference in her sister's happiness."

"Will she forgive him?"

"I wish I had some idea. She and Miss Bennet are apparently extremely close, even for sisters. But Darcy must overcome this problem if he is to have any hope at all of winning Miss Elizabeth's hand."

"How long has he been gone?"

The colonel looked up at the clock on the mantel. "Almost an hour now. Miss Elizabeth strikes me as the type of woman who would find it much easier to forgive an insult against her own person than an attack on the happiness of her sister. I suspect Darcy is not having an easy time of it."

Chapter 7

In the cool dappled sunshine of the grove, Elizabeth was warming to the discussion. "You have been the principal, if not the only means of dividing them from each other, of exposing one to the censure of the world for caprice and instability, the other to its derision for disappointed hopes, and involving them both in misery of the acutest kind! How could you have done such a thing? My sister is the kindest person in the world. What did she ever do to you, sir, to call down such retribution upon her head? And Mr. Bingley is your friend! Your best friend! He is the only person Jane ever met who might rival her sweetness of temper. And he loved her, as she did him. How could you take it upon yourself to decide that they did not deserve their happiness?!"

For a brief moment her good manners threatened to fail her; her small hands formed into fists at her sides and she had an urge to strike him. She was shocked to experience such an uncivilized impulse and resolved to control herself better. She had no way of knowing that her words were worse than blows to him.

"Miss Elizabeth. Please. I know I am in the wrong. I have

come to you to apologise. Please, may I speak?"

She spat out a surprisingly harsh rejoinder. "Have not your words done enough damage already?"

He winced. "I acknowledge the damage I have done. It appears that I was entirely in the wrong. May I please speak?"

She was a little embarrassed by the rawness of her anger, her lack of courtesy to this man who truly seemed remorseful and was, for reasons opaque to her, trying to apologise. *He is still the best chance of Jane ever seeing Bingley again. I will listen.*

"Yes, Mr. Darcy, I regret my outburst. Please continue."

"Your reaction is entirely natural and not unexpected. But I have more to say, and I thank you for the opportunity to say it. I had not been long in Hertfordshire, before I saw, in common with others, that Bingley preferred your eldest sister, to any other young woman in the country. But it was not till the evening of the dance at Netherfield that I had any apprehension of his feeling a serious attachment. I had often seen him in love before. At that ball, while I had the honour of dancing with you, I was first made acquainted, by Sir William Lucas's accidental information, that Bingley's attentions to your sister had given rise to a general expectation of their marriage. He spoke of it as a certain event, of which the time alone could be undecided. From that moment I observed my friend's behaviour attentively; and I could then perceive that his partiality for Miss Bennet was beyond what I had ever witnessed in him. Your sister I also watched. Her look and manners were open, cheerful and engaging as ever, but without any symptom of peculiar regard, and I remained convinced from the evening's scrutiny, that though she received his attentions with pleasure, she did not appear to be encouraging him in any way. I studied her for some time and she did not have the look of attachment about her."

Elizabeth made a small sighing sound. *What was it Charlotte had said?* *"In nine cases out of ten, a woman had better shew more affection than she feels. Bingley likes your sister undoubtedly; but he may never do more than like her, if she does not help him on."* She sighed again.

Darcy looked at her for a long moment and when it appeared that she was not actually trying to speak, he continued.

"Your superior knowledge of your sister suggests that I must have been in error. If it be so, if I have been misled by such error, to inflict pain on her, your resentment has not been unreasonable. But I shall not scruple to assert, that the serenity of your sister's countenance and air was such, as might have given the most acute observer, a conviction that, however amiable her temper, her heart was not likely to be easily touched."

"But if as you say you believed that her heart was not touched, how could he be in any danger from her, beyond some temporary disappointment?"

He took a deep breath. "That is an excellent question. I come now to the most difficult part of my explanation." He took another deep breath. Elizabeth looked at him apprehensively.

"Pardon me, Miss Elizabeth, I do not wish to offend you further, but I feared that under the influence of your mother, Miss Bennet might accept my friend's hand for reasons unrelated to affection."

"Because he is rich."

"Yes, that is one possibility, or perhaps because she wished an establishment of her own, or some other combination of reasons. But I would not wish a loveless marriage on my friend, especially considering his open and caring character. It would crush his spirit."

"And you believed my mother capable of --"

Here Elizabeth stopped. All the memories of her mother's loudly voiced boasts and indiscretions at the Netherfield ball and other social occasions came flooding back into her mind, and from actual weakness she sat down upon a nearby log and took her face into her hands. Jane's happiness, destroyed in large part by her own mother's bad manners! *What is Mr. Darcy to me, pray, that I should be afraid of him? I am sure we owe him no such particular civility as to be obliged to say nothing he may not like to hear."* Elizabeth remembered it all vividly, with full rations of shame and horror, and felt the weight of her embarrassment a hundredfold from the night it had all happened, just a few hours before Bingley had left Hertfordshire never to return.

Darcy looked on in helpless silence for a few seconds. Finally he could remain silent no longer.

"Miss Elizabeth, are you unwell?"

"I am not ill, if that is your question." She raised her head, finally, and looked at him. Her eyes were suspiciously shiny but her voice was controlled.

"I am glad to hear that. Perhaps that is the best I can hope for at this moment."

"What now, Mr. Darcy?"

This was the question he had been grappling with for the past 24 hours. He knew he needed to follow where she led.

"I beg your pardon, Miss Elizabeth?"

"What now?" He detected a note of irritation in her voice. "You have explained yourself most completely, and while I disagree entirely with your actions and consider them officious and overbearing, I cannot claim that I lack understanding of your motivations."

"I thank you for that."

"So, what now? You have acknowledged that you were in the wrong. What amends are you going to make? You have offered me an apology and an explanation. But I surmise that you have not yet apologised to Mr. Bingley, and yet it is he and Jane who have been the most wronged by your actions."

"I do owe as much to Bingley. May I have your permission to disclose any part of what you told me today about Miss Bennet's feelings?"

Elizabeth stopped to think for a moment. She did not want Jane to be humiliated or exposed, and yet she felt somehow that Bingley was to be trusted with this information. She was less certain about Darcy, but he already knew everything there was to know. "Yes, Mr. Darcy, you may tell him. May I rely upon your discretion to not expose Jane excessively? If you discover that Mr. Bingley no longer cares for her, please say as little as possible. And please do not disclose Jane's tenderest feelings to Miss Bingley. I do not trust her."

"You need not concern yourself with Miss Bingley. I would not dream of including her in this discussion." He paused for a moment and then continued, "I do not trust her either." *You have no idea how little I trust her.*

This unexpected additional bit of frankness surprised Elizabeth, and she met Darcy's look of concern with a wry half-smile. "Very well, then, sir, I am glad to find that we agree on something."

"We agree on at least a few things, I hope, beginning with the fact that my arrogance created a terrible threat to the happiness of two very kind, gentle souls who deserve better."

She nodded.

"I will ride to London this afternoon to see Bingley."

"So soon!"

"Have I not waited too long already?"

"Since you mention it, yes."

"And so I am off. Do not be surprised to hear that Bingley has discovered a sudden need to visit Hertfordshire."

"And what a shame that would be, since Jane is in London."

"Your sister is in London? Yes, of course she is. I remember your mentioning it. Where is she staying?"

"She is with our aunt and uncle Gardiner in Gracechurch Street, number ___."

"In that case I predict that Bingley may see fit to pay a call on her as early as tomorrow morning."

"You seem very confident of Mr. Bingley's inclinations."

"We will know very soon whether I was correct."

"Thank you, sir. I must return to the parsonage now. We have been here for quite a long time."

"Miss Elizabeth ..."

"Yes, Mr. Darcy?" She looked up and met his eyes. That unrecognizable emotion was back.

"I know you have been very angry with me, and I richly deserved it. May I ask whether there is any hope of your accepting my apology and perhaps forgiving me for my actions?"

Elizabeth frowned. "I find this question to be somewhat premature. I do not mean to keep you in suspense, Mr. Darcy, but I cannot say for sure until I have heard from Jane. It is mostly on her account that I have been angry. If Jane emerges happy from this terrible episode I shall find it much easier to forgive."

"Fair enough. Then I shall have even more motivation to secure a good outcome. Thank you, Miss Elizabeth." He took up her gloved hand and bowed over it, brushing his lips against it and pressing gently.

"I wish you safe travels, Mr. Darcy."

Their eyes met and she pondered again what she saw there.

"It is not a long trip. I shall be back tomorrow."

And he was gone.

Elizabeth felt a kind of warm tingling all over her body. She thought perhaps it was simply residual excitement from the very animated conversation she had just taken part in, but in that case she might have expected it to wane over the next few hours, and it did not. It was anticipation. Anticipation for Bingley's reaction to Darcy's apology; anticipation for sweet Jane, pining away in Gracechurch Street, not knowing that Bingley might be there to see her the very next day. Perhaps even a tiny portion of anticipation for herself, although she knew not what for.

Chapter 8

By the time Darcy strode into the library at Rosings he had already planned out the next twenty-four hours in some detail. "Richard! I will ride to London this afternoon to see Bingley. You must make my excuses to Aunt Catherine, as I do not expect to return in time for dinner tonight. If I leave London early tomorrow I should be back by midday.... Anne!" He bowed. "My apologies, Cousin, I did not see you."

"Obviously not," she replied. "Is there anything I might do to help you?"

"Your mother will not be pleased that I have left even for less than a day. Please tell her I had an unexpected matter of business come up that I needed to handle personally in London, but that I should be back before teatime tomorrow. I think that is all the explanation we need provide."

"But, Darcy," Richard interjected. "Is it well? Are you well? Was your walk fruitful?"

"I am going to see Bingley and apologise to him for my actions. If he is kinder to me than Miss Elizabeth was, I should be well."

"Was she so very angry?"

"Yes. Yes, she was. I – I am glad that is over. I thank you, Richard, for making me aware that it was necessary. Not only because it is a relief to speak an overdue apology, but because I was truly in the wrong, which I did not understand until Miss Elizabeth helped me to see it, and I need to make it right. And although it was important to apologise and explain to Miss Elizabeth, it is imperative that I make my confession to Bingley."

Darcy glanced over at Anne, who was watching them both attentively. "I look forward to having Miss Elizabeth as a cousin," she said. He turned to look pointedly at Richard, then looked back to Anne. "I had observed some unusual behaviour from you and forced Richard to tell me what was about. Please do not be angry with him."

"I can never be angry at Richard for very long."

"I depend upon that, Cousin," Richard replied, as Anne broke into a giggle.

"In any event, I am for London. Richard, do you plan to call at the parsonage later today?"

"Would you like me to?"

"Yes, I think so, mainly to observe."

"May I come along?" Anne's cousins looked at her with surprise. "I am sure I would enjoy a social outing. We can take my phaeton."

"Very well, then," said Richard. "We shall call at the parsonage later."

Darcy bowed to them both and departed.

**

"Bingley! So good of you to receive me at this hour."

"Darcy! Of course. I am glad to see you, but I confess your arrival is quite unexpected. I understood that you were in Kent with Colonel Fitzwilliam visiting your aunt."

"Yes, I am – or, rather, I have been – and I will return to Kent tomorrow. But there is something I need to tell you, and frankly, I feel it cannot wait."

Bingley's smile faded. "What? Has there been some kind of accident or mishap?"

"No, no, do not concern yourself. It is not bad news. But I owe you an apology."

The door opened and Caroline Bingley swept into the room, having received intelligence from a housemaid that her quarry had been admitted to the house. "Mr. Darcy! What a lovely surprise. We have not yet had tea. Will you join us?"

Darcy and Bingley looked at each other. Finally Darcy spoke. "You are very kind to invite me, Miss Bingley. But I have come to discuss a matter of some importance with Charles and had not planned to stay." Miss Bingley was all curiosity but could only nod.

The gentlemen rose. "Please excuse us, Caroline." Bingley led Darcy out of the drawing room and down the hall to the study, where they would not be interrupted. He closed the door and after a searching look at Darcy, went to the sideboard and poured them each a brandy. "Sit, my friend. It is obvious that you are very unsettled. Whatever it is, I am ready to hear it."

Darcy settled into a wingbacked chair, sighed, and took a sip of brandy, then another sip. Bingley gazed at him sympathetically, waiting.

"I was wrong about Miss Bennet."

"About Miss Bennet! What were you wrong about?"

"She did care for you. Very much. It is possible that she still does."

"She cared for me? Darcy, how can you possibly know this?"

"Her sister Miss Elizabeth is in Kent, visiting her friend, the one who is married to my aunt's parson. She got an idea," he prevaricated, "that I had a part in your decision to leave Hertfordshire. And she abused me at some length about it."

Bingley grinned as he imagined Miss Elizabeth berating his friend. "I do not understand how you came to be discussing this subject with Miss Elizabeth, but I am very glad to hear it. Really, this is excellent news, Darcy. Why should you be so distressed?"

"I have a confession to make to you, Charles."

"Yes?"

"Miss Bennet has been in London these three months. She called here once. To my eternal disgrace, I conspired with your sisters to keep this knowledge from you. Your sisters delayed their return call for weeks and then returned the call only to cut their acquaintance with Miss Bennet. I knew this too."

Bingley was no longer grinning. In fact, Darcy had never seen his easygoing friend so angry. "Let me make sure I understand. Miss Bennet called at this house and was not received as a valued friend? My sisters did not extend even the most basic courtesies to her? And you collaborated in this, and in keeping this knowledge from me? Why, Darcy, why? How could you?"

Darcy looked down and took another sip of brandy. "Bingley, I came here to apologise. And I do apologise, most abjectly. I was completely in the wrong. I was trying to protect you because of my belief that she did not truly care for you, but having learned that I was mistaken, I came here to give you this information, to extend my apologies, and to make whatever amends I can."

"How long have you known this?"

Darcy pulled out his pocket watch. "About seven hours."

"What, you just found out this morning?"

"Yes, Miss Elizabeth *enlightened me* just this morning." He grimaced.

Bingley laughed. "Perhaps the real question is who was

unkinder to you, me or Miss Elizabeth?"

"I would have to say that she was, Charles. She is fiercely loyal to her sister."

"And speaking of that lovely sister, Darcy, you let slip a very important piece of information. She is still in London?"

"Yes. This is what I meant when I said I wanted to make amends. She is staying with her aunt and uncle Gardiner in Gracechurch Street, number ____."

"And she cares for me, Darcy? She truly does? She would welcome my call?"

"If Miss Elizabeth is to be believed, and I do believe her, her sister cared about you very much and was strongly affected by your departure from Hertfordshire. Miss Elizabeth certainly implied that her sister's affections are still engaged, but I cannot make any promises. You will have to go there and endure whatever awkwardness may have been created. But I am optimistic, based on Miss Elizabeth's account of the situation."

"Well, then, I think that you and I need to pay a call on the Gardiners in the morning."

"You feel I should come along? Why?"

"I might need a witness, Darcy! I might need someone who can confirm that I did not know she was in London until just now."

"Has Miss Bennet been called to the bar in recent months? Do you fear she will cross-examine you under oath?"

"I just want her to know that I came as soon as I could."

"Very well."

"But tonight, I must confront Caroline."

"I think you should wait until tomorrow, Charles, after Miss Bennet can give you her account of exactly what transpired, and then you will know what to say to your sister."

"That is a good idea. But I cannot resist letting slip to Caroline that I have just learned from you of Miss Bennet's presence in London, and that I am going to call on her tomorrow. If Caroline knows what is best for her she will confess voluntarily. But I do not think she will. She will try to talk me out of calling on Jane – Miss Bennet. But I shall and I must. And you SHALL come with me."

"So I shall."

"And now, Darcy, will you stay and have tea with us? Perhaps we can tell Caroline now that we plan to call on the Gardiners tomorrow." Bingley was grinning again as he rubbed his hands together in anticipation.

Darcy knew that he was uncommonly indebted to his friend's goodwill for the forgiveness that had been extended to him, and as much as he dreaded the idea of tea with Caroline Bingley, it was his duty to remain. Bingley rang the bell and asked for tea to be served in the drawing room, and the two friends walked slowly in that direction.

Miss Bingley appeared in the drawing room a few minutes later, just as the tray was being brought in. She immediately busied herself with preparing tea for her brother and Darcy and served them with her best domestic flourish.

"Mr. Darcy, we are so happy to see you – aren't we, Charles? – but I do wonder what brings you to London right now. We were under the impression that you were visiting your aunt in Kent."

"Yes, I have been, and I will be returning to Kent tomorrow, but I came to give Charles some information that I knew he would be interested in, and which I only learned earlier today."

She looked at both of them expectantly. Finally Bingley spoke. He chose his words carefully.

"Jane Bennet is in London, Caroline. Is that not good news? Darcy and I are planning to call on her tomorrow morning."

Alarm flashed in Caroline's eyes. She glanced at Darcy. He inclined his head.

"Mr. Darcy, Charles, this is such a surprise. I thought we were *all* in agreement that Miss Bennet did not return Charles' affections and that it was best for *everyone* if we did not see her again." Darcy could not mistake her meaning.

"Perhaps we were mistaken in our impression, Miss Bingley. In fact, I have come to believe that we were quite mistaken."

"I hardly think that likely, Mr. Darcy. You are such an exceptional judge of character. Do you not recall observing that Jane smiled too much?"

"Do not say another word, Caroline!" interjected Bingley. "I am very much looking forward to seeing Miss Bennet tomorrow and hearing from her about how she has been passing her time in London. I wonder how long she has been here." He looked directly at his sister, who was fidgeting. "It will be good to see her."

"Please excuse me," gurgled Caroline, and bolted from the room.

When the door slammed shut behind her, Darcy and Bingley looked at each other for a moment and burst into laughter. Darcy recovered first. "Bingley, perhaps you should not be too severe on your sister. Remember that I was aware of everything she was aware of, and to my shame I collaborated with her and Mrs. Hurst in this matter."

"No, Darcy, you are different. Caroline and Louisa were strictly worried about our social status. I know that even if you were mistaken, your principal objective was my well-being. But I would like to ask you a question."

"Of course."

"Exactly how was it that you happened to embark on such a sensitive topic with Miss Elizabeth? How could it possibly have come up? Do not mistake me, I am delighted that it did, but it seems almost improper, somehow, for the two of you to have such a discussion."

"Oh, Charles."

"What? It is a simple enough question."

"My cousin Colonel Fitzwilliam made me aware that Miss Elizabeth was angry with me because of my role in separating you from her sister."

"But how could she know about it?"

"Colonel Fitzwilliam told her."

"He told her!? And he knew because --"

"Because I told him that I believed that through my efforts you had been saved from marriage to a woman who did not love you."

"And he told Miss Elizabeth because—"

"He did not know that the woman he spoke of was her sister. He told her because he knew she did not have a good impression of me and he wanted her to know what good care I take of my friends."

Bingley regarded his friend sympathetically for a moment and then began to laugh again. "Oh, Darcy. How you have paid for your mistake."

You do not know the half of it, my friend. And I hope you never will.

Chapter 9

By agreement Bingley presented himself at Darcy House the next morning so that he and Darcy could travel to Gracechurch Street together. They climbed into Darcy's coach and embarked on the three-mile ride to Cheapside without much conversation. Bingley was as subdued as Darcy had ever seen him, and Darcy was wondering how Miss Bennet would receive them, and how she would describe the visit to her sister. Finally they arrived at the elegant, well-kept townhouse that matched the address Elizabeth had provided. A distinguished-looking butler of middle years opened the door and accepted their cards, returning a moment later to say that the ladies were at home.

Bingley's heart was pounding as he and Darcy were escorted into the drawing room. The ladies rose to greet their callers and there she was, even more beautiful than he remembered. He bowed deeply. She curtseyed and cast down her eyes. He was without words and for once it fell to Darcy to observe the social niceties for both of them. "Mrs. Gardiner, Miss Bennet. We are very happy to find you at home."

Madeline Gardiner's good manners smoothed over the initial awkwardness. "Please sit down, gentlemen. We are happy to receive you. I will ring for tea." As she did,

Bingley boldly stepped toward the chair closest to Miss Bennet's and claimed it. She looked up at him for a second, smiled shyly, and looked down again. Darcy placed himself near Mrs. Gardiner and offered a smile of his own. *Elizabeth is going to hear all about this call. Make a good impression on her favourite aunt.*

"Mr. Darcy," his hostess began. "While it is a pleasure to meet you, it is also a surprise. I have been under the impression that you were in Kent these recent weeks. Have you any news of my niece Elizabeth?"

He should not have been surprised or startled by this commonplace question, but he was. He wondered how much emotion he was showing. "Your niece Elizabeth. Yes, I have seen Miss Elizabeth many times in recent days. She is quite well."

"I am glad to hear it. Her letters suggest that she has enjoyed her visit to Kent very much."

"Miss Elizabeth appears to delight in the walking paths of Rosings Park."

"Yes, and she has written to us of her pleasure in the society she has enjoyed, including you and your cousins."

Henry! Has she written to her aunt about Henry?

"Miss Elizabeth is a delightful companion. I am sure I can speak for all of my cousins as well as myself in saying that we have enjoyed our time with her." *Except for yesterday morning. That was not really enjoyable. Necessary, but not enjoyable.*

He quickly glanced at Bingley, who was speaking earnestly

with Miss Bennet in low tones. She was blushing but did not appear distressed. Mrs. Gardiner followed his look and sighed.

"Mr. Darcy, I do not wish to put you in an awkward position, but may I be candid?"

"Please, Mrs. Gardiner, I welcome your frankness." He tugged at his cravat, which seemed tighter than it had when he had dressed a few hours earlier.

"Very well, then. Can you help me account for Mr. Bingley's presence here? Jane called on Mr. Bingley's sisters three months ago and was met with disrespect and discourtesy. First they told her they had not received her note advising them of her presence in town, and then they waited several weeks to return the call, and did so only to cut the acquaintance." Darcy knew all this, but hearing it from Mrs. Gardiner's lips filled him with shame in a way even Elizabeth's words had not. "So I am quite unable to understand the reasons for his sudden appearance here," she concluded.

"Mrs. Gardiner, I cannot tell you everything, but I will tell you what I can."

She nodded.

"Bingley is here today because he learned of Miss Bennet's presence in London only yesterday afternoon."

"But his sisters—"

"His sisters did not desire a connection with the Bennet family. They did not disclose to Charles that Miss Bennet was in London."

"And he found out just yesterday --?"

"From me. I in turn had learned of Miss Bennet's disappointment just yesterday myself, from Miss Elizabeth. Realizing the importance of this information, I rode to London right away to let Bingley know what I had learned. He asked me to come along on this call so that if necessary I could attest to the truth of the account I just gave you. I am grateful to you, ma'am, for allowing me to provide this information."

She smiled conspiratorially. "I am glad to have been of service." Looking over at his friend, she added, "Mr. Bingley?"

He looked away from Jane with some difficulty. "Yes, Mrs. Gardiner?"

"I would like to invite you and Mr. Darcy to be our guests for dinner tonight, if you are not otherwise engaged. I know that my husband would very much like to meet you both."

"It would be my pleasure to join you, but Darcy will have to speak for himself."

"I promised my family that I would return to Kent this afternoon, Mrs. Gardiner. I am very sorry to decline your hospitality but it cannot be helped. In truth, it is probably time for us to take our leave now."

Bingley looked stricken.

"Do not feel you must leave on our account," Mrs. Gardiner offered. "We have no particular engagements today."

"Here is my suggestion, Bingley," Darcy said. "I will take my carriage home and prepare to ride back to Kent. After the carriage brings me home, it can return for you, in perhaps another hour or so. Would that suit?"

"Yes, Darcy, and I thank you."

"Very well, then, I shall return to Kent. Miss Bennet, Mrs. Gardiner, have you any letters or other items you would like carried to Miss Elizabeth? No? Then I shall be off."

Mrs. Gardiner saw him to the door personally. "Thank you, Mr. Darcy, for what you have done for my niece."

"I hold Miss Bennet in the highest esteem, and I believe that she and Bingley are well suited. I am glad they are having their chance to become reacquainted, especially without his sisters at hand."

"I understand you very well, Mr. Darcy. Thank you again."

***

Darcy arrived at Rosings shortly before teatime, exhausted but relieved, and entered from the back door nearest the stables in the hope of gaining his rooms without having to account to anyone. *There was so much that could have gone wrong today, and yet it did not. I wonder how Bingley fares. I need a hot bath and a brandy, not necessarily in that order.*

"Darcy!" Thank God it was only Colonel Fitzwilliam.

"Quiet, Richard!" Darcy hissed, gesturing toward the

drawing room with his head.

"Sorry. How did it go?"

"Could we talk later, please? I want a bath very badly."

"Yes, but you will want to talk with me before you see Aunt Catherine."

"Have tea brought to my rooms in three quarters of an hour."

"Very well."

"Darcy! Darcy, is that you?" The imperious tones of Lady Catherine were heard from the drawing room. Darcy bolted up the stairs with a nod to Fitzwilliam. "Where have you been?"

Richard approached his aunt. "Darcy has gone upstairs to refresh himself after his journey. He will see us at dinner."

"His *journey*! Why was it necessary for him to go haring off to London so abruptly? This is quite unlike him."

"Aunt Catherine, please. He will be at dinner and I'm sure he will tell us as much as he is able."

Harrison arrived with the tea tray just as Darcy's valet Perkins was tying his fresh cravat, and Colonel Fitzwilliam was close on the footman's heels. As the door closed behind the servants Darcy devoured a tea sandwich in two bites and sighed at his cousin, although his satisfaction was apparent. He bolted two more tiny sandwiches, took a long sip of tea, and leaned back in his chair with his eyes closed, wrung out from the physical and emotional exertions of the last two days.

The colonel took a sandwich and observed his favourite cousin with compassion. "Shall I leave you alone to rest for a while before dinner, Darcy? You look spent."

"No, no, Richard, that would not be helpful. I fear that if I allowed myself to rest now, I would not wake till morning." He opened his eyes and straightened slightly in his chair.

"Very well, then. I see that you are not bleeding and therefore I surmise that Bingley did not call you out."

"Bingley! Bingley may be the son of a tradesman, but he is as good and gentlemanly a man as I have ever known. He understood immediately that despite the wrongness of my judgment I had acted in what I perceived to be his best interest. We called on Miss Bennet together this morning, and she was properly reserved but obviously very happy to see him. And he could hardly tear his eyes away from her. It is within the realm of possibility that they are already engaged. In any event it will not be long."

"So he has forgiven the deception."

"Well, he has forgiven *me*, but I do not think he will forgive his sisters so quickly." Darcy barked a short laugh. "In particular it appears that Miss Bingley has reason to fear her brother's wrath. I do not envy her."

Richard Fitzwilliam grinned. It was amusing to imagine Caroline Bingley being brought to heel.

"But Richard, you said I needed to speak with you before encountering Aunt Catherine at dinner."

"Yes."

"I take it she was displeased by my absence."

"Quite. But she responded to your departure by inviting the parsonage party to dinner last night, and haranguing us all at length after dinner about the necessity of Anne keeping you in line when the two of you are married."

"In front of the Collinses and their guests?!"

"Of course."

Darcy bit back an oath. "So now Miss Elizabeth thinks I am truly engaged to Anne?"

"Well, Cousin, that was the interesting part. After Aunt Catherine's monologue, Anne invited Miss Elizabeth to sit with her for some time. Her excuse was a piece of needlework but they did appear to be chatting very amicably. There is no telling what Anne said to her. But it is unlikely that Anne would have said she was engaged to you."

"And Anne knows everything now, about my intentions?"

"Yes. I think she wishes to make herself useful, and that tete-a-tete might have been the beginning of her campaign on your behalf."

"I am not sure how I feel about that. Anne is not always tactful or discreet. She is her mother's daughter, after all."

"All the more reason for you to take control of your own destiny and win Miss Elizabeth without Anne's help. You have ten more days until Henry returns."

"Only ten days…. But I do have some very good news to deliver to her tomorrow morning." Darcy allowed himself a smile as he settled back into his chair.

Even his aunt's merciless questions and harangues at the dinner table that evening could not affect the inner satisfaction Darcy felt knowing that he had been the instrument of restoring Jane Bennet to Bingley, and vice versa. He excused himself early, in need of rest, and slept more peacefully than he had in months.

Chapter 10

Anne was up early for breakfast with her cousins on Day 4. It was clear that she now expected to be treated like a full participant in their scheme, and the support she could offer was too valuable to decline. Yes, she and Miss Elizabeth had done some needlework together after her mother's admonitions to Anne to keep Darcy in check after she married him. Yes, she had made a point of telling Miss Elizabeth cheerfully that she and Darcy were not engaged and had no wish or intention of ever being married to one another. Miss Elizabeth's reaction was harder to describe. She did seem interested in Anne's disclosure, even perhaps a little grateful to Anne for bringing it up. But beyond that she had said little. Anne confessed that she had highlighted Darcy's best qualities during that hour together: his intelligence, his loyalty to his family and friends, his integrity and determination, his oft misunderstood reserve. Miss Elizabeth had listened to all of that, then simply observed that Darcy's character was puzzling to her, and Anne let it drop.

This was not half bad, her cousins felt. In fact it might be excellent groundwork for the next conversation Darcy would have with Elizabeth. Richard was enthusiastic.

"Well done, Anne! Don't you agree, Darcy?"

"Yes, I must agree, Anne, that was a fine hour's work. Thank you. And now I am off for … my morning walk."

"Good luck, Cousin." Anne's and Fitzwilliam's voices rose in a chorus of wellwishes.

Back into the park Darcy embarked, an uncommon lightness in his step as he reflected on all that had happened since his last conversation with Elizabeth. He headed for what he now knew to be her favourite path, and after a few minutes saw her. "Miss Elizabeth!"

She turned toward him and there seemed to be authentic pleasure in her countenance. She might even have been looking forward to seeing him. "Mr. Darcy! Good morning!" Even though he knew that she was truly eager only for news of Bingley and Jane, he let that smile warm his soul for a moment before responding.

"I thought you might like to hear about my trip to London." He smiled back at her and held out his arm, which she accepted. *This feels so right and good.* They walked a half-minute in silence.

He cleared his throat and began. "I called on Bingley the day before yesterday."

"I am glad to hear it. I am certain he was happy to see you."

"I was afraid he would never want to see me again after I informed him of my actions and my conversation with you."

"Yet, knowing Mr. Bingley, I would surmise that you are still the best of friends."

"Bingley is a very good man." They walked a few more steps. "He did insist that I accompany him on a call in Gracechurch Street yesterday."

She stopped walking and turned until she could see his face. "Please tell me the whole story from beginning to end." She gestured at a nearby bench.

They sat, and punctuated by her questions, he did.

"So Mr. Bingley spent more than an hour with Jane and then returned for dinner yesterday?" Elizabeth's eyes were shining.

"I believe so. In any event, that was the plan when I left him at the Gardiners'."

"Mr. Darcy, I thank you from the bottom of my heart for what you have done in the past two days."

"Miss Elizabeth, as you know, it was the least I could do to remedy the grievous wrong I had committed. I hope you now understand that my actions were intended only to protect my friend. I made a terrible mistake, and I have done my best to undo it, or at least undo its effects."

"And I do thank you for that. Now I must wait to hear from Jane, and perhaps my aunt. They will have the most recent information." They stood and she dusted off her skirt. She glanced up at the sun. "Heavens! It is so late. Charlotte will be very worried about me. I hope she has not sent out a search party." She curtsied deeply and reached out her hand. He seized it with an eagerness that startled her, bowed over it, and brushed his lips against her gloved fingers. "Good day, Miss Elizabeth." After a long second she tugged gently and he released the hand, then gazed after her as she moved toward the parsonage.

***

On Day 5 of the campaign it rained, long and hard. The inhabitants of Rosings remained indoors. Darcy and his cousins breakfasted together and agreed that there was little to do but wait for news of Miss Bennet and Bingley. Darcy and Fitzwilliam made some progress on the ledgers each day, but all the outdoor work had to be suspended. Accustomed as they were to walking and riding the grounds daily, both men became restless by dinnertime, and retired early.

The rain showed no sign of abating, so on Day 6, by careful management of Lady Catherine during the evening meal, her daughter and nephews contrived for Her Ladyship to agree that if it were still raining at breakfast time a note would be sent inviting the entire party from the parsonage to dinner the next day. After the point was won, Anne made a point of saying how much she was hoping to do needlework with the ladies, and the colonel remarked that he hoped Anne would spare Miss Elizabeth enough time to play the pianoforte for them.

Darcy, naturally, was silent.

The rains continued into Day 7 and so a dinner invitation was duly carried to Hunsford, with a prompt acceptance. Darcy and his cousins – for Anne was now an integral part of the plot – spent the day in the library, where Anne took an active interest in the ledgers and other estate business. Darcy did his best to concentrate on the work, and not dwell on the pleasure and pain he anticipated from the evening to come, but in truth all the cousins were distracted. After Anne was summoned to attend her mother shortly before teatime, Fitzwilliam worked silently for a few minutes, until he glanced up and saw Darcy staring out a window, his expression blank. The colonel's heart ached for his rich, handsome cousin, whose privileged early life had not prepared him for the trials he was currently undergoing, but who was meeting the challenge with impressive perseverance. Darcy remained by the window, oblivious, as his cousin approached him quietly.

"Darce. Do you want to talk? About tonight? About anything?"

Darcy started at his cousin's close approach. "No! – Perhaps. – I don't know, Richard. I don't know if it would help me or not. I feel we have canvassed this subject fairly extensively between us. I do wish I had more insight into Miss Elizabeth's thinking."

"By now she has probably had a letter from her sister, don't you think?"

"Oh, yes, and based on the way Bingley looked, it is possible that they are engaged by now." A faint smile of satisfaction touched his lips.

"So that is excellent! Surely Miss Elizabeth's forgiveness will be complete when she knows her sister's happiness is secured."

"You know how much I hope for that... and yet..."

"And yet what?"

"I cannot escape the feeling that there is something else standing between Elizabeth and me. I do not know what it is, but there is something."

The colonel chuckled. "Elizabeth, is it? Well, perhaps tonight you will be able to discover what it is."

"If I am brave enough."

Miss Elizabeth would be so surprised if she could see the effect she has had on my cousin. "Of course you are brave enough. You have acknowledged that you love her. We both agree that she is an exceptional woman and would suit you very well, both as a wife and as mistress of Pemberley. Whatever it is must be something relatively small, some kind of misunderstanding. I know how introspective you are, so if after all this time you do not know what it could be, it is not something you said or did wrong, but more than likely some faulty information Miss Elizabeth has picked up along the way. But you cannot combat it until you know what it is."

"I suppose you are right."

"You know I am right. And now you have six days remaining to accomplish your objective."

"Only six days! However can I do it?"

"Darcy! Calm yourself. Think about everything you accomplished in just the first four days. That was immense progress. You will get there with time to spare."

"I hope you are right, Cousin."

Not desirous of encountering Lady Catherine, the cousins had tea on a tray in the library and returned to their ledgers, although little was accomplished before it was time to change for dinner. Darcy went up early for a hot bath to calm his nerves, and dressed with unusual care before joining his aunt and cousins in the drawing room a few minutes before their guests were expected. Outside the many expensively glazed windows of Rosings, the rain continued to fall.

Murdoch, Lady Catherine's butler, announced the arrival of the Hunsford party at precisely the appointed time. Lady Catherine nodded her approval as her guests filed in, bowed and curtseyed, and made their way to seats. Darcy's breath caught for a moment as he looked at Elizabeth. She was wearing a pink sprigged muslin dress that emphasized her creamy complexion and sparkling eyes, and she was smiling. *At me? Is she smiling at me?* It appeared so.

Colonel Fitzwilliam, observing the exchange of glances, grinned at his cousin.

"Mr. Collins! I commend you on your punctuality! You know that I expect it."

"Yes, Lady Catherine, you have been so good as to explain to me many times—"

"Miss Bennet. You will play for us after dinner."

Elizabeth looked away from Darcy to his aunt. "Of course, Your Ladyship, if that is your wish."

Lady Catherine directed the conversation for a few more minutes until dinner was announced. Darcy seized the moment and stepped toward Elizabeth, holding out his arm to escort her to the dining room. He knew without looking that Richard was doing the same for Lady Catherine and Anne. Elizabeth looked up at him and smiled brilliantly. He wondered if she could feel his racing pulse through the sleeves of his shirt and coat.

"Have you any news from your sister, Miss Elizabeth?"

"Hmmm, well, Kitty writes that she has a new bonnet." *She is teasing me again. This is wonderful.*

"I think you know that I was asking about a different sister, Miss Elizabeth."

"Yes, Mr. Darcy, since you ask, it happens that I do have news of another sister. It seems that Mr. Bingley has proposed to Jane, and she has accepted him!"

I knew it. And I am so very glad that I need not endure Miss Bingley's ranting on the subject. "That is excellent news, Miss Elizabeth. I shall write to Bingley to wish him joy."

"I know he told Jane he was going to write to you here, but perhaps he has not yet had a chance to do so."

"Bingley is a dreadful correspondent. But I hope that news this good will bestir him to greater diligence."

As the meal was served and conversation ebbed and flowed around the table, he watched her covertly. Her face was so animated most of the time, and yet, he observed, she maintained a steely control over her facial expression during periods when Lady Catherine was speaking. At the moment she was talking with the colonel. He said something that made her laugh and she raised her napkin to cover her mouth, but her eyes were dancing with amusement. As much as he loved looking at her, Darcy experienced this moment as both pleasure and pain. He was glad to see her happy and obviously enjoying herself, and at the same time he could not help envying his cousin's greater ease in company.

At the end of the meal Darcy and the colonel, with a sharp look at Mr. Collins, insisted to their aunt that there was no reason to enforce the separation of the sexes after dinner, and the entire party returned to the drawing room and began to take seats within the orbit of Lady Catherine's favourite chair. To the amazement of her cousins, Anne immediately and forcefully took Elizabeth by the hand, speaking quietly, and drew her to a sofa on the other side of the room where the large piece of needlework was pulled out again. This development surprised Lady Catherine almost as much as it did her nephews.

"Anne! Of what are you and Miss Bennet speaking? I must have my share in the conversation!"

"Nothing important, Mother, we are talking about choosing colours of thread."

"I hope Miss Bennet will not forget that we wish her to perform."

"Pray do not be concerned, Your Ladyship. I shall be happy to play whenever you like."

For the next half hour Darcy surreptitiously watched the young ladies while making monosyllabic responses intended to convince his aunt that he was conversing with her. He could tell that Richard was doing the same. It soon became clear that the ratio of stitching to conversation on the sofa was extremely low and, more disturbing yet, Anne seemed to be dominating the discussion. *Oh, no. She is trying to help me. How can I stop her?*

"Miss Elizabeth!"

Anne stopped talking and both ladies looked up.

"Yes, Mr. Darcy?"

"Would you be willing to favour us with some music now?"

"I would be delighted." She smiled apologetically at Anne, tied off her threads, and moved toward the pianoforte.

Fitzwilliam rose. "May I turn the pages for you, Miss Elizabeth?"

"Yes, thank you, that would be very kind."

As Elizabeth began to play, Darcy stepped toward Anne. "Cousin, please tell me what you and Miss Elizabeth were talking about."

"Why, Darcy, are you asking me to violate any confidences?"

"Hardly, as it appeared that you were the one doing most of the talking."

"Fair enough. As you might have surmised, we did spend some time speaking of you."

That is exactly what I was afraid of. "And..."

"Miss Elizabeth does not understand you very well."

"Does she ... dislike me?" Darcy held his breath.

"No, I think it is safe to say that she does not dislike you *now*."

Well, this is progress, I suppose. "But she does not like me yet?"

"I think she does, or at least she wants to, but ..."

"Yes?"

"She has taken in some ... incomplete information about you."

"That's a curious word. Incomplete. I have tried to give her the fullest possible view of my character. From what source did this incomplete information come to her?"

"From your old steward's son, George Wickham."

"How did that shameless cur impose on her?" The volume of his voice rose for a moment until he caught himself and hissed the rest in a fierce whisper. Luckily the music camouflaged the worst of it, and Reverend Collins' conversation distracted Lady Catherine and Maria. Darcy's fists clenched involuntarily and he looked imploringly at his cousin. "What did he tell her, Anne? What did he say to her?" *If he uttered a single syllable about Georgiana, I will kill him with my own hands.*

"I do not know exactly, but it was something about your

father's will, that you somehow deprived Wickham of his rightful inheritance."

Oh, that. I know how to handle that. Darcy took and squeezed his cousin's hands. "Thank you, Anne. Thank you so much. This is very helpful. Now I know what I have to do."

Across the room Lady Catherine gazed at them appraisingly, but said not a word.

Elizabeth was now playing a piece she knew by heart, so she had excused the colonel from page-turning duty. Noticing the gleam in his aunt's eye, he hastened to his cousins. "Beware, Cousins, for Lady Catherine is watching you closely and she appears ready to have the banns read." Both dropped their hands as if they had been burned.

A somewhat desultory general conversation ensued. Shortly the carriage was summoned to return the Hunsford party to the parsonage, and the cousins and their aunt retired to their rooms.

A sharp rap on Darcy's door heralded the fully expected arrival of Colonel Fitzwilliam. Seated by his fire in pyjamas and dressing gown, Darcy was ready. "Will you join me in a drink, Richard?"

"You read my mind." The colonel, likewise informally attired, accepted a seat and two fingers of brandy. He took a sip and sighed. This was the good stuff, Darcy's private stock, not the swill Lady Catherine kept on hand. He took a second, bigger sip. "So tell me, Cousin, what exactly transpired between you and cousin Anne? Your conversation appeared ... quite animated."

"Anne had acquired some valuable intelligence in her conversation with Miss Elizabeth."

"Relating to…"

"Wickham."

"Wickham?!" Colonel Fitzwilliam sat bolt upright. "What has HE to do with this?"

"You will recall that I mentioned seeing Wickham in Hertfordshire, where he had joined a local militia."

"Yes."

"Well, during that time, he had many opportunities to be in company with Miss Elizabeth and the rest of the neighbourhood."

Fitzwilliam looked grave. "And presumably many opportunities for mischief."

"Yes. And he apparently regaled her, and others, with some tale of my cheating him out of his rightful inheritance. Anne could not provide any more detail."

"Please let me kill him, Darcy. I know exactly how I would do it, and no one would ever be the wiser."

"Richard, no. But now I know that there is at least one more vital conversation I must have with Elizabeth before there is any chance she would agree to a courtship. And I am running out of time."

The colonel decided to ignore Darcy's use of only the lady's Christian name.

"Nonsense, you still have six days."

"But if the rain continues, less than that."

"Look out the window. The sky is clear now, and the moon is bright. This augurs well for tomorrow." He took a final swig and set down the empty glass. "I will see you at breakfast, Darcy."

Darcy only nodded, distracted. The colonel let himself out quietly and tiptoed down the hall to his own rooms. Darcy would not find sleep for another hour.

Chapter 11

Despite their late night, Darcy and Fitzwilliam met for breakfast at their usual early hour. As they filled their plates from the sideboard the colonel asked, "Darcy, is it your plan to inform Miss Elizabeth about Wickham's attempt on Georgiana?"

"I have been pondering it since last night, and to be honest, Richard, I do not know if I should. Do you have an opinion about it?"

"My first thought was that you should not do so under any circumstances, but now I am not so sure. Of course I want to protect Georgiana more than anything, but I also have strong trust in Miss Elizabeth's discretion, and if you need to tell her about it in order to make her understand just how vile he is, then perhaps you should."

Darcy took a sip of his coffee before replying. "This will be a delicate conversation in any event, but yes, I do trust her profoundly. After all, I am prepared to offer her all that I have."

"I cannot wait to welcome her into the family, Cousin. And not as a sister."

Darcy laughed shortly. "Four days after today. Can I do it?"

"Yes, you can, and you shall. Look," he gestured at the windows, "it is a beautiful day. A perfect morning for a walk. And a good talk."

Darcy poured a third cup of coffee, dropped in two lumps of sugar, and stirred it absently. He was physically and emotionally exhausted. Wholly unaccustomed to the recent levels of self-criticism and self-reformation he had experienced, he could not remember a week of his life, ever, when he had conceived and uttered so many apologies — not even when he was a boy, taking the blame for George Wickham's transgressions. This was worse, since these acts of contrition arose from his own willful misconduct. But it was also more than a little thrilling, because the reward might be a lifetime of happiness with a woman of quality, a woman he adored, a kind of woman he had imagined but never knew existed. He drank his coffee, hoping it would help him keep his wits about him for the critical conversation he needed to have this morning. His cup drained, he accepted his cousin's best wishes and set out on his morning walk.

Just a few minutes later Anne joined the colonel in the breakfast room. "Have I missed him?"

"Yes, he has gone for his walk."

"Godspeed to him. I hope he can convince her of his worth. She will be the making of him if he can win her."

"Agreed, and I truly believe that she and Henry would not suit at all."

"Henry!" Anne snorted in a very unladylike way. "Henry is a good fellow but he has not touched a book since he left Cambridge. They would be a disaster together. Although their children would be beautiful."

The colonel chuckled. "I am sure that Darcy could also give her some very handsome children."

"And would very much enjoy doing so."

"Anne!" The colonel was shocked.

"What, do you think I do not know about these things? Do not be so naïve, Richard. I can read Darcy's countenance when he looks at her and at times it is pure desire. It is a wonder that she has not noticed it."

"Because of the rude remark he made on the evening when they were first in company together, I think she has never considered the possibility."

"She is a highly intelligent woman, but she does not understand Darcy very well."

"I do think Mrs. Collins has noticed. But either she has kept her own counsel about it, or Miss Elizabeth has not believed her."

Anne buttered a muffin. "What say we pay a morning call on the parsonage?"

"Without Darcy?"

"Precisely. I would like to observe Miss Elizabeth's demeanor in the aftermath of their conversation."

"To what end, Anne?"

"Idle curiosity, perhaps? Or perhaps some useful intelligence we could bring back to Darcy?"

"Very well. Let us set out at half past ten. Shall we take your phaeton?"

"Yes, I will have it brought around at that hour. Thank you, Richard."

***

"Miss Elizabeth!"

She knew the voice behind her very well. "Mr. Darcy." She turned and curtsied. "Are you taking your walk this morning, sir?"

"Yes, as I see you are. May I join you?" He offered his arm and she took it. They began to walk in companionable silence as he pondered the task of correcting her information about George Wickham.

"Miss Elizabeth, do you recall my mentioning that I felt I owed you two apologies and an explanation?"

"Yes, although I would say that in fact you have given me two apologies and two explanations."

"That would not be an unreasonable way to characterize our conversations." They continued walking. "What would you say if I told you that it appears I may owe you a third explanation?"

"But not an apology this time! Should I be offended, sir?"

She is teasing again. Perhaps this will not be too bad.

"No apology this time, but I do believe you need to hear an explanation relating to my family's relationship with Mr. Wickham."

"Mr. Wickham!"

"Yes. I am given to understand that whilst in Hertfordshire he very industriously spread an account of having been wronged by me in some way relating to my father's will."

She looked up in surprise. *Is he now to overturn my last grudge against him? How wrong is it possible for one person to be about another?*

She was blushing harder than he had ever seen her blush. He noticed the blush and wondered if her feelings for Wickham ran deeper than he had thought. His heart felt seized in an icy grip at the possibility, but he plunged ahead.

"Please allow me to lay out the facts of our relationship. Of what he has particularly accused me I am ignorant; but of the truth of what I shall relate, I can summon more than one witness of undoubted veracity. Mr. Wickham is the son of a very respectable man, who had for many years the management of all the Pemberley estates; and whose good conduct in the discharge of his trust, naturally inclined my father to be of service to him, and on George Wickham, who was my father's godson, his kindness was therefore liberally bestowed. My father supported him at school, and afterwards at Cambridge;—most important assistance, as his own father, always poor from the extravagance of his wife, would have been unable to give him a gentleman's education. My father was not only fond of this young man's society, whose manners were always engaging; he had also the highest opinion of him, and hoping the church would be his profession, intended to provide for him in it. As for myself, it is many, many years since I first began to think of him in a very different manner. The vicious propensities—the want of principle which he was careful to guard from the knowledge of his best friend, could not escape the observation of a young man of nearly the same age with himself, and who had opportunities of seeing him in unguarded moments, which my father could not have."

He dared a sideways glance at her. The blush of a few minutes ago was gone. She was pale. He continued, his voice flat and unemotional.

"Here again I shall give you pain—to what degree you only can tell. But whatever may be the sentiments which Mr. Wickham has created, a suspicion of their nature shall not prevent me from unfolding his real character. It adds even another motive. My excellent father died about five years ago; and his attachment to Mr. Wickham was to the last so steady, that in his will he particularly recommended it to me, to promote his advancement in the best manner that his profession might allow, and if he took orders, desired that a valuable family living might be his as soon as soon as it became vacant. There was also a legacy of one thousand pounds. His own father did not long survive mine, and within half a year from these events, Mr. Wickham wrote to inform me that, having finally resolved against taking orders, he hoped I should not think it unreasonable for him to expect some more immediate pecuniary advantage, in lieu of the preferment, by which he could not be benefited. He had some intention, he added, of studying the law, and I must be aware that the interest of one thousand pounds would be a very insufficient support therein. I rather wished, than believed him to be sincere; but at any rate, was perfectly ready to accede to his proposal. I knew that Mr. Wickham ought not to be a clergyman. The business was therefore soon settled. He resigned all claim to assistance in the church, were it possible that he could ever be in a situation to receive it, and accepted in return three thousand pounds. All connection between us seemed now dissolved. I thought too ill of him, to invite him to Pemberley, or admit his society in town. In town I believe he chiefly lived, but his studying the law was a mere pretence, and being now free from all restraint, his life was a life of idleness and dissipation. For about three years I heard little of him; but on the decease of the incumbent of the living which had been designed for him, he applied to me again by letter for the presentation. His circumstances, he assured me, and I had no difficulty in believing it, were exceedingly bad. He had found the law a most unprofitable study, and was now absolutely resolved on being ordained, if I would present him to the living in question—of which he trusted there could be little doubt, as he was well assured that I had no other person to provide for, and I could not have forgotten my revered father's intentions. You will hardly blame me for refusing to comply with this entreaty, or for resisting every repetition of it. His resentment was in proportion to the distress of his circumstances—and he was doubtless as violent in his abuse of me to others, as in his reproaches to myself. After this period, every appearance of acquaintance was dropt. How he lived I know not. But last summer he was again most painfully obtruded on my notice. I must now mention a circumstance which I would wish to forget myself. Having said thus much, I feel no doubt of your secrecy."

"Mr. Darcy, please, rest assured that I do believe you. Please do not feel obligated to violate any confidences." Her distress was palpable.

"I thank you for that, Miss Elizabeth, but I think it is important for you to know all, so that perhaps he can be prevented from imposing on other innocent young women in the future."

"Very well, then. Please continue. I will not interrupt you again."

"You may feel free to interrupt me at any time. I want you to understand, and it may help you to ask questions.

"My sister, who is more than ten years my junior, was left to the guardianship of my mother's nephew, Colonel Fitzwilliam, and myself. About a year ago, she was taken from school, and an establishment formed for her in London; and last summer she went with the lady who presided over it, to Ramsgate; and thither also went Mr. Wickham, undoubtedly by design; for there proved to have been a prior acquaintance between him and Mrs. Younge, in whose character we were most unhappily deceived; and by her connivance and aid, he so far recommended himself to Georgiana, whose affectionate heart retained a strong impression of his kindness to her as a child, that she was persuaded to believe herself in love, and to consent to an elopement. She was then but fifteen, which must be her excuse; and after stating her imprudence, I am happy to add, that I owed the knowledge of it to herself. I joined them unexpectedly a day or two before the intended elopement, and then Georgiana, unable to support the idea of grieving and offending a brother whom she almost looked up to as a father, acknowledged the whole to me. You may imagine what I felt and how I acted. Regard for my sister's credit and feelings prevented any public exposure, but I wrote to Mr. Wickham, who left the place immediately, and Mrs. Younge was removed from her charge. Mr. Wickham's chief object was unquestionably my sister's fortune, which is thirty thousand pounds; but I cannot help supposing that the hope of revenging himself on me, was a strong inducement."

Elizabeth was weeping openly now, and despite a nearly uncontrollable urge to take her in his arms and kiss away her tears, he disciplined himself to stand by and watch her. *She believes me. She will never credit his words again.*

After a few moments she looked up, clutching her handkerchief. "Such a villain! And we believed him. I believed him. Mr. Darcy, it is I who owe you an apology now."

"No, no, Miss Elizabeth," he reassured her, handing her his own handkerchief, as hers was now soaking wet. "It is not at all surprising that he was able to deceive you. Ignorant as you previously were of every thing concerning him, detection could not be in your power, and suspicion certainly not in your inclination. Wickham is a practiced seducer. In a way, I have long envied his ease in company, but I cannot regret the other differences between us."

"Of course not."

As she calmed, he wondered what to say next. He had not planned beyond this moment. But he had awakened, and perhaps emboldened, her native curiosity.

"Mr. Darcy, I need to return to the parsonage now, but I also need to know, why are you telling me these things?"

"Why?"

No need to panic. Thank God, I will have a day to sort out what to tell her.

"Yes, why? I certainly appreciate what you have done for Jane, more than I could ever tell you, and I also appreciate your apology for your words at the Meryton assembly. But this? To expose such a painful episode in your family's history to me? I am grateful, sir, and I appreciate the honour of your confidence. But I do not understand why."

He took her hand, ungloved since she had been wiping her eyes with her handkerchief, bowed over it, and kissed it lightly. "I wanted you to know the truth."

Chapter 12

Again and again on the walk back to the parsonage, she berated herself. *How could I have been so gullible, so stupid? How could I have been so blind to the impropriety of Wickham's telling me all those things within a half hour of our first being introduced? How did I not notice that while he was claiming that out of respect for the father he would never expose the son, in fact that was exactly what he was doing? Was he that artful, as Mr. Darcy says, or was I that credulous? I, who have felt so proud of my discernment, am really just another silly girl, not much better than Lydia. I was prejudiced against Mr. Darcy because he had insulted my appearance, and eager to believe Wickham because he flattered me. I am ashamed of myself.*

When the house came within view she stopped, took several deep breaths, blew her nose into her own handkerchief, then pulled out Darcy's. Moving to the water pump, she pulled a few ounces and dampened Darcy's immaculate linen with cool water to refresh her eyes and cheeks. That done, she ran her fingertips slowly over the FD embroidered in one corner in elegant blue script and wondered again whether she would ever understand this perplexing man.

Entering the house through the kitchen door, she greeted Charlotte's housemaid Sally and asked where Charlotte would be found. "Mrs. Collins and Miss Lucas gone out to do an errand in town, Miss."

Concealing her relief, Elizabeth thought she might go to her room and think for awhile, but as she was removing her bonnet and spencer, the door knocker sounded and a moment later she could hear the voices of Colonel Fitzwilliam and Miss de Bourgh in the entry hall. There was no polite escape available now, so she stuffed Darcy's damp handkerchief into her reticule and entered the parlour to receive the visitors.

"Miss de Bourgh! Colonel! How nice to see you. Sally, will you bring some tea, please?"

The visitors took seats on the settee opposite hers and studied her closely. She did not quite appear her usual self. Her smile did not reach her eyes and those eyes looked a little shiny, but she carried on as if all were normal. "I am terribly sorry that Charlotte is not here to receive you, but she has gone on an errand to the village, and in fact I myself just returned less than five minutes ago from a long walk in the park."

"We are likewise sorry that Darcy could not accompany us on this call, but he too went out this morning for a long walk in the park, and had not yet returned when we left Rosings.... Did you happen to see him whilst you were walking?" Anne was not sure what kind of response she was hoping for, but the blush that suffused Elizabeth's face and shoulders confirmed the answer she expected. Now, would Elizabeth admit it?

"Yes, it is almost comical, Rosings Park is so large, and yet I have come upon Mr. Darcy several times in the park during my visit. We have had some very interesting discussions."

Sally entered with the tea tray, and Elizabeth bent to the preparation and pouring. Anne and her cousin exchanged glances. Elizabeth was not trying to conceal her encounters with Darcy from them. Yes, they knew her to be an honest and forthright person, but usually a woman being courted informally would be a little more coy about it.

The same thought occurred to both of them at almost the same moment. *She has no idea he is courting her.*

Colonel Fitzwilliam took up the conversational reins after a sip of tea. "Oh, yes, now that you say it, Darcy has mentioned that he has encountered you in the park in recent days. He enjoys his conversations with you very much."

"I could not have said for certain that he did or did not. He is not an easy man to understand."

"Yes, and no. He is very reserved with people he does not know well. He is fundamentally very reserved in company. He has endured the attentions of many people who are more interested in his wealth and influence than in him as a person. But at the same time there is something very artless about him. He is a man of very deep commitment to principle. He tells the truth and always does his duty, whether it is against his inclination or not. I do not know a better man."

Anne added her own insights. "As you know, my mother

has been going on for years about my supposed engagement to Darcy. Neither of us desires such a connection, and we never have. In truth, I have no desire to be married to anyone, ever. But I know that if I did, I could never find a better man than my cousin."

Elizabeth knew she needed to respond. "I am grateful for the time I have spent with your family here at Rosings, because I confess that I misjudged your cousin harshly based on his time in Hertfordshire, and it is clear to me now that he is a very good kind of man. And since his particular friend, Mr. Bingley, will soon be my brother, it would be a terrible shame if I had allowed that misjudgment to persist. I blush to think of it even now.

"Speaking of brothers, Colonel, have you had word from the viscount? He has been gone for a few days now."

DRAT. Is she just making conversation now, or does she really care about Henry?

"No, Miss Elizabeth, Henry has always been a terrible correspondent, and I'm quite certain that he is enjoying his visit to Featherdale so much that the thought of taking time to write to his brother has not occurred to him."

"I can easily believe that. It is difficult to picture him at a desk."

"I agree. Henry is a good man but he has always preferred field sports, riding, and even cards and billiards to reading and correspondence."

"He is very different from Mr. Darcy in that way," Elizabeth observed.

"Yes, Darcy is the most diligent of men."

Anne chimed in, "Even at Rosings, he always has an escritoire placed in his rooms and he spends at least an hour a day on correspondence with his steward, solicitors, and naturally his sister Georgiana."

For Elizabeth, even this seemingly offhand mention of Georgiana brought back a flood of recollections of the morning's disclosures. She blushed again, although neither of her visitors quite understood why at first, until she spoke. "I have heard many good things about Miss Darcy. I gather she is very accomplished and also very sweet and innocent."

He told her. Good man. "Yes," said the colonel, "I am joined with him in Georgiana's guardianship. For many years he has been both brother and father to her."

"Does that make you her mother, Colonel?" Elizabeth's voice was neutral but her eyes were alight. Anne, startled, laughed out loud in a way Lady Catherine would certainly have disapproved of.

The colonel, too, taken by surprise, gave a hearty laugh. "No, Miss Elizabeth, I would not quite put it that way. I do not think she would want my advice about fashions and hairstyles."

"But she might want or even need your advice about men, do you not agree?"

He looked at her and she at him in a moment of perfect comprehension. *Yes, she knows, and she understands. Darcy needs to marry this girl even more than I thought. Georgiana could do with such a sister.*

Anne was rising. "Miss Elizabeth, I have so enjoyed spending this time with you, but I think it is time we returned to Rosings."

"Of course, Miss de Bourgh, I hope you have not become overtired."

"Not at all. And, please, when we are out of my mother's presence, I hope we can dispense with these irksome formalities. I would like you to call me Anne. May I call you Elizabeth?"

"It would be an honour."

"I do not meet many ladies of my own generation, Elizabeth, but I like you very much, and I hope we can be friends. Perhaps we can even correspond after you leave Hunsford."

"I would be delighted."

"Excellent. I hope that we will be able to call on you again. Please tell Mrs. Collins how sorry we were to miss her."

"I certainly shall. And I shall hope to see you here again whenever you are up to it."

With an exchange of proper curtseys and a bow, the callers departed.

Knowing that Charlotte was due home at any moment, Elizabeth told Sally that she was going to lie down for a brief rest before the midday meal and repaired quickly to her room. She had far too much to think about to risk any conversation with her dangerously insightful friend.

Driving back to Rosings in the phaeton, Anne and her cousin were dissecting the visit with zeal.

"Richard, you never told me what Darcy's plan was for this morning."

"This morning he told her about his family's relationship with George Wickham."

"Wickham! The Pemberley steward's son?"

"Yes, he appeared in Miss Elizabeth's neighbourhood at roughly the same time as Darcy last fall. He had joined a militia that was quartered in the nearest town, and he began to spread scurrilous slanders about Darcy withholding from him a preferment from his father's will."

"Oh, yes, Miss Elizabeth mentioned last night that she had heard something to this effect. If she believed him, perhaps she is not as insightful as we think."

"No, remember, Wickham is a sly mischief maker, and also Darcy had made a terrible impression on the neighbours. They thought him arrogant, proud, snobbish, and determined to be above his company. So Wickham's story was perfectly consistent with the beliefs of those who had met Darcy only recently."

"What a tangle!"

"Yes, and Darcy realised none of this before he left Hertfordshire."

"Speaking of Darcy," Anne added as her cousin handed the reins to one of the Rosings grooms, I am sure we will find him in the book room, and he undoubtedly wonders what has become of us. Let us join him at once."

Darcy, as his cousins surmised, had been seated at the master's desk in the Rosings library for a half hour, with two large ledgers open in front of him, neither of which could hold his attention. *Tomorrow. What am I going to say to her tomorrow? Should I propose marriage? Would it be safer to ask for a courtship? Can she truly have not understood what I have been about, and why? Will she be surprised? Might there be anything else she holds against me? Perhaps it might rain tomorrow? Yes, that is what I need. Thunder and lightning, and torrential rain, to keep everyone indoors for another day, so I can plan.*

WHERE IS RICHARD? WHERE IS ANNE? Where are they when I need them?

"Cousin!" The colonel's voice boomed as he and Anne entered the library. She closed the door behind them with great care. It would not do for her mother to overhear any of this.

"Where have the two of you been? I have been looking for you."

"We decided to call on the parsonage this morning."

"To what end?" Darcy's voice was sharp.

"It was my idea, Cousin." Anne stepped forward and sat down in one of the chairs that faced the desk. I thought it might be useful to assess Miss Elizabeth's state of mind after her morning walk."

"And what did you discover?"

"She does not appear to be aware that you are courting her!" exclaimed Anne.

"I am not surprised. This morning after I told her about Wickham she thanked me and then asked me why I was telling her all these things. Then she needed to return to the parsonage, so I was granted another day to sort out what to say to her. But you are correct, she does not seem to know or even suspect my design."

Anne nodded. "She is so intelligent, but she does not understand you at all."

"Remember, the very first words she ever heard me speak were a slur on her appearance."

"That is what Richard told me, Darcy. What on earth possessed you to be so rude?"

"Please, Anne, I have berated myself quite extensively on that account and do not require additional criticism. I would give anything to take that back, but it is too late now, and at least I have apologised."

Richard rubbed his hands together. "So, she has no idea that you love her and want to marry her. Splendid. How do you plan to deliver the news tomorrow morning?"

"I was rather hoping for rain," Darcy muttered.

"Come, Cousin." Anne did her best to look stern. "Let us be methodical about this." She stood up and began to pace back and forth in front of the desk.

"Methodical? That does not sound very romantic," the

colonel objected.

"There is time enough for romance tomorrow," Anne insisted. "What he needs is a structured plan to fall back on."

"I think that Anne has a point." Darcy stood up and stretched out his stiff back muscles. "Part of my problem is that when I am with Elizabeth, I sometimes become so flustered that I cannot think of what I wanted to say. A plan would be helpful."

"Elizabeth, is it?" Anne laughed and seemed about to speak again, when Harrison entered with a silver tray. "You have received a letter from Featherdale, Colonel."

Fitzwilliam tore it open and began to read. He looked up at his cousins after a few moments. "Henry is considering returning a few days early. He will write again to let me know his exact intentions. So, Darcy, you might need to pull yourself together sooner than expected, perhaps even tomorrow, if you want to secure Miss Elizabeth's hand before her titled admirer arrives." He winked.

Darcy paled and sat down.

"Tomorrow."

"Possibly tomorrow. So, yes, Cousin, let us make a plan," Anne replied.

Chapter 13

The early morning sun streamed in through the open windows as Darcy woke. In his dressing room his valet Perkins was already at work. His hot bath was almost ready and the shaving implements were laid out. Within a half hour Darcy was bathed and shaved. Perkins looked mildly askance at him for rejecting the first three waistcoats he suggested, but knew better than to do more than express approval of the final selection.

Although it was very early, Fitzwilliam and Anne were already at breakfast.

"Oh, good, you are here," the colonel drawled. "We were wondering if you had lost your nerve."

"Richard, you should be ashamed of yourself!" Anne hissed.

"Yes, Cousin, you should," Darcy said. "I do not need this kind of abuse today." He turned to the sideboard and filled his plate with food. A footman entered, poured coffee, and was quickly excused.

Anne smiled encouragingly at her non-fiancé. "Are you

ready, Darcy? Is there anything else Richard and I can do to help prepare you?"

"No, I do not believe so. This is my task now. You have both been very helpful, but now I must be responsible for the rest." He drank some coffee and pushed his eggs around on his plate with a silver fork. "I know that the difficulties have been almost entirely of my own making, and so must the resolution be."

He looked up from his plate at them. "But if she refuses me, I do not know how I shall go on." He blinked and looked down again.

Fitzwilliam and Anne gazed at their cousin with sympathy. Finally Anne spoke. "Darcy, now that she knows the real you, and you have made amends for your mistakes, surely she can learn to love you, even if she does not love you now. And she is not indifferent to you. I have observed her and I can say with confidence that she certainly is not. Do not despair. Be sincere and express your feelings, and trust in Providence and Miss Elizabeth's innate good sense."

Fitzwilliam came over and clapped Darcy on the shoulder. "You can do this, Cousin! You have waited so long, and Miss Elizabeth is just the woman to breathe some life into this family. Go and get her."

Darcy took a last sip of coffee and abandoned his tepid eggs. "Right. It is a beautiful day for a walk. I shall be off now."

A minute later they watched him through the window as he strode boldly away from the house and toward his future.

***

"Miss Elizabeth!"

The familiar voice was there again. She admitted to herself that she had been hoping to hear it. She looked up and smiled. "Mr. Darcy! Good morning, sir."

"And good morning to you, Miss Elizabeth. Are you just setting out on your walk today?" He extended his arm and she took it.

"I have been out for a few minutes. I find fresh air and exercise to be good for thinking."

Thinking?! He was tempted to panic but remembered what Anne had said about Elizabeth's good sense. "Pray, if you require privacy and solitude, tell me so, and I will withdraw and leave you to your thoughts."

"Oh, no, thank you, Mr. Darcy, but that will not be necessary."

"Very well then, let us walk."

They strolled in amicable silence for a few minutes. Finally he turned to her and said, "As it happens, there is one other thing that I need to say to you."

She looked at him quizzically. "Will this be another apology? Or an additional explanation? Or some other form of communication heretofore unattempted by you, Mr. Darcy?"

She is teasing me again. YES. I can do this.

"The third, actually, Miss Elizabeth." He looked into her eyes and willed her to understand.

"Will spoken words be involved, or am I to discern your meaning by looking into your eyes?" She was smiling.

"There will be words. And when I said it would in fact be a form of communication heretofore unattempted by me, that was the literal truth. I have never proposed marriage before." Her smile faltered and her eyes widened. He stopped walking, faced her, and took hold of her hands.

Her questioning eyes searched his face. He took a deep breath, looked directly into those very fine eyes, and continued. "Miss Elizabeth, please, you must allow me to tell you how ardently I admire and love you. From the very moment of our first acquaintance I have felt a deep, passionate attraction to you, not only to the beauty of your person, but to your mind and character as well. It is true that for a time I did allow myself to be put off by the indecorous behaviour of your mother and your younger sisters, and I must confess to you now that I convinced Bingley to leave Hertfordshire not only for his sake, but for mine. I knew I was in danger of losing my heart to you if I remained in the neighbourhood for another moment. But even among all the distractions of London I could never put you out of my mind for so much as an hour. And then when I fled to the country, as I walked the halls of Pemberley I longed for your presence there with me every day. The very moment I first saw you again, here in Kent, I knew that I could never forget you, that you are the only woman I will ever love. Please do me the honour of becoming my wife."

He leaned down, brought her gloved hands together and

kissed them, but did not relinquish them. She looked at him, stunned, and wondered, *has Charlotte then been right all along? Can it really be?*

After a long moment he kissed her right hand again, and squeezed it. "You are silent. Your silence is a torture for me. But you are not running away, so I suppose that is a good sign."

She came back to herself with a jolt. "Oh, my goodness, Mr. Darcy, I had not intended to be unkind in any way. But I am somewhat surprised by this development."

"Of course it seems to me that my intentions have been obvious, but I know that there have been some very serious obstacles to our forming any kind of understanding. And yet – I hope those obstacles are gone. I hope I have removed them in a way that has been convincing and satisfying to you."

"Absolutely!" She looked up, smiling. "You have been very diligent."

"And..."

"And I am honoured by your proposal."

"That does not sound like an acceptance."

"Fair enough, but it is likewise not a rejection."

"All right, then, what comes next?"

She glanced toward a nearby bench they had sat on during one of their earlier walks, and he led her there, releasing her left hand in order to capture her right between both of his. He squeezed it gently again. She did not pull it away.

"Mr. Darcy."

"Miss Elizabeth."

"This is so sudden."

"I can see that for you it is. For me, it is the culmination of many months of longing."

"So you said."

"Please believe me."

"I do believe you, sir."

"Please believe also that my feelings are deep and sincere."

"I do not doubt them – or you."

He pressed her hand against his heart for a moment, and felt her hand tremble in his. He looked from their joined hands to her face as a soft laugh bubbled from her lips.

"Am I amusing you, Miss Elizabeth?"

Her laughing eyes met his. She looked sheepish. "I am so sorry. My mirth was not directed at you."

"Yes?"

"I was thinking about your cousins."

"And what exactly were you thinking about them?"

"They know about this, do they not?"

"This being…"

"Your proposing to me."

"Yes, Anne and Richard have been aware of my intentions for some time."

She laughed again. "That explains so much."

"Oh, no. Dare I ask … what did they say?"

Seeing the look of alarm on his handsome face, she squeezed one of the hands that was still holding hers. "It was not so bad. It is just that I was puzzled by some of the things they have said to me lately, and now it is all so obvious."

"There is one thing that is still not obvious, at least to me."

"And what is that?"

"What can I do to convince you to accept me?"

She looked down into her lap. He held his breath.

"There is nothing you can do."

He began to panic. *I cannot lose her now.*

Hearing his quick intake of breath, she looked back up at him, saw the anguish on his face, and squeezed his hand again. "Pray do not leap to awful conclusions, Mr. Darcy. I meant only that you have done everything that was within your power to do. Now it is up to me. I must take some time to consider your offer, because it was so wholly unexpected."

"May I add, Miss Elizabeth, that – " He paused. *How to word this?*

"Yes?" she smiled.

"The mere fact that you did not accept me immediately is another sign that you are the best choice I could possibly make."

"And how is that, sir?" Her voice was teasing but her question called for a serious answer.

"Miss Elizabeth, I have been pursued by marriageable young ladies and their matchmaking mothers for years. I can assure you that there is not an unmarried woman in the London *ton* who would take even five seconds to consider whether to accept an offer to become the mistress of Pemberley."

"Like Miss Bingley?" She chuckled at his momentary grimace. "With all due respect to Pemberley, sir, I would not be marrying a grand estate. I would be marrying a man. You, to be precise. That is what I need to consider."

"And that is why I know that falling in love with you is one of the most sensible things I have ever done. And why I need you to say yes ... as soon as possible."

She sat silently for a moment, then gently tugged her hand away from him. He looked at her with concern.

"I need to think, and most importantly, to return to the parsonage now. It is growing later and Charlotte will wonder where I have been. I should walk that way alone."

"Please promise me that you will consider my offer."

"Mr. Darcy, I can assure you that I will be able to think of little else."

Now it was his turn to chuckle. "Very well, then. When might I expect an answer?"

"Please let me have a day or two. I promise I will not make you wait long, one way or the other."

I wish she had not said those last few words. But I will take it.

"Thank you, Miss Elizabeth."

"Thank you, Mr. Darcy. I understand the magnitude of the compliment you have paid me today, and I am moved and flattered and deeply honoured by your proposal."

"Will you walk out tomorrow morning?"

"Surely you already know the answer to that, sir."

He inclined his head. "I suppose I do. I will rephrase my question. Would my company be welcome during your walk tomorrow morning?"

"Yes, of course."

The smile he gave her was the broadest she had ever seen on his handsome features. She could feel her knees grow weak. She curtsied quickly and headed back on the path to the parsonage before she could weaken further and fling herself into his arms on the spot.

Mr. Darcy admires me! He loves me and wants me to be his wife! How can such a thing be? Charlotte was right from the very beginning. She will be so smug when I tell her. If I tell her. If I do not accept him I must never mention this to anyone.

If I do not accept him? What am I thinking? Would I really not?

I do not know.

Chapter 14

Elizabeth returned to the parsonage and found it blessedly quiet. Her cousin was visiting with Lady Catherine and Charlotte had gone into the village with Maria. She accepted a cup of tea from Sally and sipped it reflectively. Later she heard voices from the front hall and realised that she was not equal to either Charlotte's observation or her cousin's conversation at present, so she slipped quietly up the back stairs and secluded herself in her room. At length she fell asleep, and dreamt of dark-haired children playing in a beautiful garden.

When she came downstairs Charlotte looked at her with amiable curiosity. "Are you well, Lizzy? It is not like you to need a nap in the morning."

"Oh, yes, Charlotte, I am perfectly well. I walked a long way today, and for some reason I did not sleep very soundly last night, so the nap was just the thing. I am very well now."

"I am glad to hear it. Tonight may be a late night for us because we have just received an invitation to dine at Rosings."

Here was a possibility Elizabeth had not considered. Was she to see Darcy again, so soon? What would it be like to be in company with him, knowing that just a few hours ago he had asked her to be his wife? Would he expect an answer already? He was an intelligent man and had to realise that she would not be putting herself forward tonight of her own volition. They had already made a plan to meet in the morning in any case. As she ran through the logic of her position she noticed Charlotte's puzzled gaze.

"Lizzy, you seem so thoughtful. Is there a reason you would not want to go to Rosings tonight?"

"Oh, no, Charlotte, not at all." She gave a thin laugh. "I was merely pondering which of my gowns that Her Ladyship has not yet seen will most effectively preserve the distinction of rank to her liking." She straightened her back and looked down her nose at her friend, and they both laughed freely.

Just as the friends recovered their composure Maria and Mr. Collins entered the dining parlour, putting an effective end to the moment of levity.

"Cousin! Her Ladyship must be very pleased with you! She has extended another of her benevolent invitations to dinner. We must be there at six o'clock. Lady Catherine places great importance on promptness."

Mr. Collins maintained a running commentary while they ate their midday meal, then went to his study. Elizabeth retired to a corner with some needlework. She needed to occupy her hands so that her distraction would not be obvious. It would not do for Charlotte to see her staring unseeing at a book whose pages never turned, and although she owed Jane a letter, now was not a good time to try to write something coherent.

She had too much to say, and therefore nothing to say.

Mostly, she needed to be alone with her thoughts.

***

Darcy returned to Rosings with a little spring in his step that had not been there when he set out. He had been reviewing their conversation from every angle and, while he was in an agony of uncertainty awaiting Elizabeth's reply, he felt there was nothing negative in her response, only surprise and a desire to take some time to consider his offer, both of which were entirely reasonable under the circumstances, and reflected well on her character. He had wished for an immediate acceptance, wished for her to say yes and step into his embrace, wished for an invitation to kiss her, but he felt he had acquitted himself well, and now had only to wait a relatively short time, compared to the months of agony he had already endured.

He noticed an unusual level of activity among the servants when he entered the house, but headed directly for the library to find his cousins. They would know what was going on.

Richard looked up from the first page of the letter in his hand. "Darcy! You are here! How did it go, man? Are you engaged?"

"Yes, Cousin," Anne added. "We are eager to hear your news."

"It went ... well, I would say. No, I am not engaged. You were right, both of you: she had no idea I was courting her. My proposal took her completely by surprise. But she listened with good grace and asked for a day or two to consider her response. I could hardly press her at that point."

Richard looked back down at his letter. "Of course not, and yet you may wish you had. This is an express I just received from Henry. He tells me that he has observed the great marital contentment of his friend the Duke of Norwich, and this has resolved him to seek the same for himself. The duchess is apparently a very vivacious and charming dark-haired woman, who has put Henry in mind of Miss Bennet. He is returning early for the express purpose of seeking her hand."

"No." Darcy dropped into the nearest chair.

"Yes, Cousin, I am afraid so. He will be here by dinnertime, and the parsonage has been invited to dinner. But do not despair. You have done so much to improve her opinion of you over the last two weeks, and at least now she has no doubts about your intentions and desires."

"But Henry is so charming. And he is a future Earl."

"Aye, that he is. But you are the one who has spent day after day courting her—"

"Courting a woman who did not recognize my courtship."

"...seeking her good opinion, and even ensuring the happiness of her favourite sister—"

"—after destroying that happiness first." Darcy raked his

fingers through his dark curls in agitation.

"Nonetheless, you have done the right thing by Miss Bennet and Bingley, and I believe you told us that Miss Elizabeth had forgiven you."

"She said she had."

"Then she did." Richard went back to reading his brother's letter, frowning.

Anne interjected, "Darcy, do not be foolish. Elizabeth is not the kind of woman who will swoon over Henry's title. If she were, you would not love her as you do. I told you she was not indifferent to you, and now that she knows your feelings it will be nigh impossible for her to refuse you."

Darcy was watching the colonel. "Richard, your expression is concerning. What does Henry say?"

Wordlessly, Richard stood up from behind the desk with the letter, walked over to where Darcy was sitting, and handed it to him.

"Read it yourself."

Darcy scanned the letter with increasing agitation. "He thinks he can save time by compromising her?! Is he mad? When did Henry become such a rake?"

"I do not know how to answer that question. I would never have expected this of him. It appears he believes that since it would be unthinkable for her to refuse a chance to become the Countess of Matlock, he would not really be compromising her if marriage were his objective all along."

"But why would he not take the time to even attempt to court her?"

"My father has commanded him to find a wife, and in fact I believe Father intends to suspend Henry's allowance if he does not become engaged very soon. But that is not a very good excuse, except.."

"Except for what?"

"I received a second letter yesterday. It was from my friend Thomas Dunmore, younger brother of the Duke of Norwich, Henry's host. Thomas reported that Henry had incurred very significant losses at cards last week. He also said that two unknown men who did not appear to be gentlemen had called on Henry at Featherdale, that he had not been at home to them, but that he had later been seen having a heated discussion with them at the inn in the village."

"Who could they have been?"

"I believe they were moneylenders, Darcy."

"So he is highly motivated to meet your father's conditions, and return to London a betrothed man."

"And what are you going to do about it, Darcy?" Anne was outraged. "You cannot allow Henry to marry Elizabeth. He does not care for her as a husband ought. You must stop him."

A knock on the door announced the midday meal, and the three cousins headed to the dining parlour.

Chapter 15

As she dressed for dinner and twisted up her long, thick curls into a simple style, Elizabeth gazed at herself in the looking glass. *Mr. Darcy thinks I am beautiful.* After years of her mother's negative comparisons of her looks to the loveliness of Jane, Elizabeth was unaccustomed to dwelling on her own appearance. She knew that when she dressed up for a ball or assembly she could make herself very pretty, but the idea that whilst nursing Jane at Netherfield – a time when she had given almost no thought to her appearance – she had managed to engage the admiration and love of such a distinguished man was almost overwhelming.

He is truly a very good man. He is so much better than I imagined, after shamefully allowing myself to be taken in by Mr. Wickham.

And yet despite my foolishness … he loves me.

He loves me.

Do I love him? How could I? I do not know him very well. But I have looked forward to our walks with great anticipation. If I search my conscience I know that I have taken extra care with my dress on mornings when I thought I would see him.

And he is very handsome. His touch and even his look affect me in ways no other man ever has. To have the love of such a man is ... an exciting idea.

Truly, I have quite a lot to think about.

If I said yes, I would make him very happy. It would make Jane very happy, to know that we would be married to best friends for our whole lives. It would make my mother very happy, perhaps so happy that I would rather not be there when she first learned of it. But my father! How could I explain my change of heart to him? How I wish I had been more restrained in my expressions of dislike for Mr. Darcy last fall!

Papa loves me and wants the best for me, and surely I can make him see... that it would make ME very happy! So there is my answer. I shall take Mr. Darcy aside tonight and accept him.

***

At five o'clock the Viscount Leicester was enjoying a hot bath in his rooms in the guest wing at Rosings after his dusty trip from Sheringham. He was very pleased that his aunt had agreed to invite the parsonage residents to dinner. As his valet Hopkins poured a pitcher of hot water to rinse his hair, he closed his eyes and imagined the evening ahead. Perhaps he could steal a few moments alone with Miss Elizabeth tonight and make her his! If he had to wait another day or two to accomplish his objective, then so be it, but it would be very handy to get it done tonight, so he could begin planning their future life, and make it back to Matlock House in London before his father's time limit expired, an engaged man. *No need to make a side trip to Hertfordshire first. Her father will undoubtedly be thrilled to learn that his daughter is to become a future countess.*

By a quarter past the hour he was seated in his dressing gown in the shaving chair, a steaming towel over his face as Hopkins prepared to complete his grooming. And just at that moment he heard heavy footsteps outside the dressing room, and his brother burst in.

"Henry, we must talk."

He waved the colonel away. "Hopkins is about to shave me. Can this not wait until later?"

"No. It cannot wait."

"Very well. Hopkins, I will ring when I am ready." The valet bowed and exited. Henry pulled the towel off his face and glared at his brother. "So...?"

"You must know why I am here."

"Are you trying to dissuade me from marrying Miss Elizabeth? Because you cannot. I know she is not of our sphere -"

"Our sphere be damned, Henry! Miss Elizabeth is a gentleman's daughter and therefore very much of our sphere. My concern is for your plan to (and here his voice lowered) compromise her. How can you even consider such a thing?"

"Well, I am willing to romance her, but I do not have a lot of time, Richard. Father expects me back in London in a few days. He has been pressuring me incessantly to find a bride, and threatened to cut off my allowance if I do not find a fiancée by the first of May. I cannot risk a breach with Father. I have *debts*, Richard. I planned to attend the house party in large part because I hoped to meet some eligible young ladies there -"

"And there were none?"

"No, there were several, and yet none of them compared favourably to Miss Elizabeth. I know she enjoyed our conversations before I went to Featherdale. She blushed and laughed in that way ladies do when they are flirting with you. So I thought, I can save quite a lot of time and make it happen now, so I can get back to London on time and also satisfy Father's requirements!"

"And preserve your allowance, and Father's favour."

"Of course! I am not stupid."

"Well, perhaps you are not stupid, but this is a stupid idea."

"How so?"

"If Miss Elizabeth refuses you, how can you plan to force her into marriage to you without her consent? Henry, it is barbaric."

Henry's eyes narrowed. "Do you have a more personal interest in this matter than you are revealing, Richard? Are you enamoured of Miss Elizabeth? Have you been courting her in my absence?"

"No, Henry, I have not." *And that is as close as I will come to the truth.* "But I like and respect her, and I perceive that she is not a woman who will be a happy bride if she is denied her right of refusal. If she feels coerced --"

"She will be a countess."

"That will not make her happy if her marriage is not of her choosing."

"Believe it or not, I do understand that. I am not particularly interested in allowing Mother and Father to choose a bride for me, as they have threatened to do. I would much rather choose for myself, and I choose Miss Elizabeth."

"So you are determined to deny HER right of choice, to take her against her will if necessary?"

"You make it sound so unsavoury, Richard."

"Do you love her?"

Henry Fitzwilliam laughed, a deep, rolling, mocking laugh, as his brother glared at him in disapproval. "Richard! Wherever are you getting your quaint ideas? That is wholly unnecessary. She is clever enough to be a good countess, and beautiful enough that it will be no hardship begetting heirs with her, I will say that. But love before marriage is a primitive notion. She will learn to love me, if she does not already, and I am sure that if she is a good and loyal wife, I shall grow into a deeper affection for her. Now go, this conversation is tiresome, and I need a shave before dinner. I mustn't frighten the future countess!" He laughed again and pulled the cord for Hopkins.

The residents of the parsonage were due in about a half hour.

In his own rooms in the family wing, Darcy was in an advanced state of agitation. He would have been under sufficient stress at the mere prospect of seeing Elizabeth and wondering about her response to his proposal, but knowing Henry's plans had made matters infinitely worse. After dressing for dinner he had dismissed Perkins until morning, not knowing what the evening was likely to bring. He was now pacing the substantial length of his bedchamber repeatedly until he feared he would wear a rut in the Aubusson carpet. Richard appeared and reported his lack of success in persuading Henry to act like a gentleman, and Darcy felt that it would be up to him tonight to find a way to protect Elizabeth without making her angry at his apparent presumption.

Meanwhile, Anne de Bourgh gloated quietly as her maid assisted her in preparing for the evening. *Mother can be so useful.*

At five minutes to six o'clock the inhabitants of Rosings assembled in the drawing room and by six o'clock sharp the party from the parsonage were being relieved of their hats and cloaks by Lady Catherine's staff. All except Her Ladyship stood to greet them. The newcomers bowed and curtsied and took places on the sofas, chairs, and settees that were arranged in a semicircle around Lady Catherine's chair whenever there was company. Just as

Henry was striding toward the chair occupied by Elizabeth, his aunt's sharp voice recalled him.

"Henry! Come and sit by me, nephew, and tell us of your house party."

Even a future earl was not inclined to refuse such a direct order. In the meanwhile Anne seized the opportunity to take the chair next to Elizabeth, nodding at Darcy, who chose a seat on the other side of their fair guest. Henry began to speak of the house party and the friends who had been present, while Anne made a show of searching for a particular piece of embroidery in her sewing basket, and not finding it. When Henry paused in his account Anne rose and said, "Excuse me, mother, my embroidery must be in my chambers. I will go to fetch it. Miss Elizabeth, will you accompany me?"

Elizabeth, confused, knew not what to say at first. She did not wish to antagonize her cousin by affronting Lady Catherine, but for once the lady did not appear to be in any mood to be affronted. "Yes, yes, get on with you both," she admonished, and Elizabeth followed Anne out of the room whilst Darcy and Richard looked at each other in wonder.

As Anne and Elizabeth approached Anne's chambers, Elizabeth tried to ask her what she was about, but Anne only placed a finger to her lips and hurried Elizabeth along until they reached Anne's sitting room. Only after they were inside, and Anne had turned the key in the lock and checked the apartment for servants, did Anne turn to her and speak.

"You are in danger."

"DANGER? How can I be in danger? From what or whom?"

"Elizabeth, I am going to tell you something that you will not wish to believe. But you must believe me. My cousin Henry has returned early for the express purpose of marrying you."

"What?" Elizabeth grabbed at the arm of a nearby chair and sat down hard.

"He apparently saw some good examples of marital felicity whilst visiting his friends and decided that it was time for him. Also, his parents are pressing him to marry. So he wrote to Richard and said he was coming back to marry you."

"But we do not have that kind of relationship. Neither of us has ever expressed that kind of interest in the other. And --"

"And Darcy proposed to you this morning."

"Yes." Elizabeth blushed. "I had almost forgot that you and the colonel knew all about it. But the viscount does not, does he?"

"No. And you did not accept Darcy, did you?"

"No, I did not. I told him I needed time to think about his offer."

"That is not unreasonable, but if you are not engaged then Henry will consider you fair game."

"Even so, he cannot possibly court me so quickly."

"He does not believe that he needs to court you."

"That sounds rather sinister."

"It is. If you do not respond to his first advances, he plans to save time by compromising you, on the theory that he can make you a countess, and you will forgive him."

"Anne. You cannot be serious. Perhaps there has been some mistake or misunderstanding."

"I am sorry to say that there has not. Henry wrote very explicitly of his plan to Richard. Richard informed Darcy and me this morning. That is why I told you that you are in danger."

"How can he be stopped? What can I do to protect myself?"

"So you do not wish to be a countess?"

"No, I do not." She blushed. "I have recently come to the conclusion that I would rather be Mrs. Darcy than anything else."

"Were you planning to tell Darcy tonight?"

"I was hoping to find an opportunity to do so, yes."

"Here is the situation. You know that my mother has not yet given up her hopes of a match between Darcy and me, even though neither of us desires such a match."

"Yes. And speaking of your mother, why was she so accepting of your pulling me out of the drawing room before dinner?"

"Elizabeth, as you may have noticed, my mother is an exceedingly proud woman who can be predictable in certain ways. When I told her that Henry wanted to find a way to get you alone this evening, she was appalled, not by his rakish behaviour, but by the idea that a future Countess of Matlock might come from a family such as yours. She is ferociously opposed to any match between Henry and you, and was happy to conspire with me to frustrate his designs on you, at least for now."

Elizabeth was astonished at Anne's revelations. "But she will be very displeased by my engagement to Mr. Darcy."

"Aye, that she will, and she will probably express severe regret that she did not just let Henry have you."

"So how shall we manage the dinner hour and then the rest of the evening?"

"My mother will do her best to keep Henry by her side all evening. If he is polite, you are safe. If he abandons her to sit and talk with you, even in full company, then you are at risk because there is nothing to stop him from taking you in his arms and kissing you in front of everyone, or compromising you in some other way, and binding you to him."

"Even if I resist?"

"I have no way of predicting how determined he will be. It is possible that if tonight seems too difficult he will seek you out at the parsonage in the morning. But my advice to you is to find a discreet moment tonight to accept Darcy as quickly as you can. Once Henry learns that you and Darcy are engaged, I hope he will desist. If he does not, I fear that Darcy will call him out, and it would destroy the family if one of them were to kill the other on the field of honour."

Elizabeth's blood ran cold at the very thought of such an eventuality.

There was a knock on the door. One of the footmen was calling them to dinner. They rose and went downstairs, knowing better than to be tardy in responding to the summons.

Chapter 16

Dinner was a tense affair with sparse conversation, carried mostly by Colonel Fitzwilliam and Charlotte, with occasional interminable interjections by Mr. Collins. The viscount and Darcy were placed at Lady Catherine's right and left, and Elizabeth was grateful to be seated two seats away from the viscount, as far away as she could have hoped for given the size of the group. The separation of the sexes was brief that evening, or at least seemed brief to Anne and Elizabeth. The latter was consumed with dread. It was unlikely that Colonel Fitzwilliam could have worked very effectively on his brother with Mr. Collins as an audience, so she knew she would need to be on her guard until she was safely returned to the parsonage.

In accordance with her chosen mission as Elizabeth's protector for the evening, Anne was ensconced with her on a double settee, embroidery on their laps, when the gentlemen entered. Lady Catherine once again called to Henry to come and sit by her, as she had just recalled that she was acquainted with the mother of one of the young lords who had been in attendance at the house party. Henry, although visibly annoyed, obeyed. Darcy and the colonel moved toward the settee occupied by Anne and Elizabeth, and took up positions on either side. Elizabeth looked up at Darcy with the warmest smile she could muster. He looked down at her with that now-familiar emotion in his eyes, and she wondered that she had taken so long to recognise it.

Yes, she mouthed at him. *Yes.*

Afraid to believe his eyes, reluctant to think his luck could have changed so much so quickly, Darcy only stared at her.

She tried again. *Yes.*

"Miss Elizabeth!" Henry Fitzwilliam was speaking.

She looked at the viscount warily. "Yes, milord?"

"I was hoping you would favour us with some music. I will turn the pages for you." He smiled ferally and stood up, bowing to his aunt and smoothing the creases from his trousers. The last thing she wanted was to be trapped on a music bench with Henry Fitzwilliam. He could do anything he wanted to her there, and she would be powerless to prevent him. She looked up at Darcy again, and then looked over at Anne and the colonel. Elizabeth was not a woman given to panic, but in the moment, she had no idea what to do.

Luckily, she was sitting next to Anne de Bourgh, who had a needle in her hand.

"OUCH!" Elizabeth cried, as Anne plunged the sharp point into her thumb.

"Oh, my goodness, Miss Elizabeth, I am so very sorry!" Anne said, pulling out her handkerchief and applying it to Elizabeth's wound. "I hope I have not ruined your gown!"

There were a few drops of blood on her skirts, but nothing too very bad. "I am sure it will all come out," Elizabeth reassured her. "Please do not be concerned."

"But you will certainly not be able to play the pianoforte tonight," said Anne, meaningfully.

"Why, no." Elizabeth smiled at her in perfect understanding. "No, I should not attempt it." She looked up at the viscount, who was staring in disbelief at the bloody handkerchief she held. "I am very sorry, milord, but it will not be possible for me to play tonight."

Now that it was clear that Elizabeth was not badly injured, the colonel and Darcy were concealing their amusement only with great difficulty.

Lady Catherine was uncharacteristically quiet, muttering only, "Anne, you must be more careful."

At this point the Viscount Leicester decided that he had had a long day and would retire. He bowed to all present, indicating that he might call at the parsonage in the morning after he had had some rest, and took his leave. Shortly the party broke up and a carriage was called to return Mr. and Mrs. Collins, Maria, and Elizabeth to Hunsford, whilst Mr. Collins fretted about whether the blood from Elizabeth's thumb would stain Lady Catherine's carriage cushions during the five minute drive back to his house.

Before the carriage could be made ready, Darcy, eager to

confirm the substance of the word that had been on Elizabeth's lips a few minutes earlier, bent over her injured hand as if to pay his respects. But when she looked up at him with glistening eyes and whispered the word audibly, it was all he could do not to pull her into his arms in front of everyone, not excepting his aunt and her idiotic parson.

"You have made me the happiest of men," he whispered back.

"Please protect me from your cousin," she replied, and he knew she did not mean that she feared another attack from Anne.

"I shall. Perhaps we should make an announcement."

"That could be unwise. Your aunt will be very unhappy with both of us."

Suddenly Anne was leaning into their conversation. "Leave Mother to me."

Careful to avoid Anne's embroidery, Elizabeth took Anne's hand in hers and said, "I must remember never to cross you, Anne."

Anne only smiled. She had a plan. She always had a plan.

After they returned to the parsonage and first Maria and then Mr. Collins retired, Elizabeth detained Charlotte in her sitting room to acquaint her with the day's events. Charlotte, however tempted to proclaim that she had been right all along about Darcy, listened respectfully without interrupting, until Elizabeth repeated Anne's disclosures about the viscount's intentions.

"What a rake!" she exclaimed. "I could never have imagined it! How can we protect you from his designs?"

Elizabeth had been obsessed with this question since Anne's disclosures. "As much as I hate to contemplate it, I shall not walk out in the morning. It is too dangerous. If I should encounter the viscount in the park, all would be lost. I shall remain indoors. If he calls, you should tell him that I have gone out because I felt the need of a walk. A long walk. A very long walk. Perhaps then he will go out to search for me, and it will be safe for me to receive Mr. Darcy here and make a real plan."

The friends embraced before finding their beds.

Knowing Henry Fitzwilliam's penchant for sleeping well past ten in the morning, his brother and cousins called at the parsonage at half past nine. Mr. Collins was visiting a parishioner and so they were received in a relaxed and jovial manner. Darcy took his longed-for place on a settee next to Elizabeth and held her hand for a moment before releasing it.

Anne was focused on strategy: "We need to get Elizabeth and Darcy out of Kent today."

The colonel agreed. "Henry needs to return to London by tomorrow if he is to meet my father's time limit. He will become desperate to compromise Miss Elizabeth if she remains in the neighbourhood and he cannot get to her. I cannot predict what he is capable of, but it is safe to say that none of us want to find out."

Darcy was still angry. "He shall not succeed. I shall call him out if I must."

Taking Darcy's hand again, Elizabeth cried, "No! Do not even think it."

"I shall do as I must," he replied reflexively, then, seeing her strong emotion, he continued, "but we will find a way to avoid that necessity." He squeezed her hand reassuringly.

Anne continued calmly, "I believe the best course of action is for Elizabeth, Darcy, and me to leave for London right away. I can tell Mother than Miss Elizabeth's thumb was becoming painful, red, and swollen, and that when I told Darcy I was concerned, he offered his carriage to take her to his London physician. I then offered to accompany them as a chaperone." She looked up expectantly.

Elizabeth was grateful but hesitant. "But Anne, will your mother not be very angry? What will she say to you?"

"She will say nothing at all. I will leave her a note and we will depart without speaking with her. How quickly can you be ready to leave?"

Before Elizabeth could respond, the door knocker sounded, and in a few seconds the voice of Henry Fitzwilliam boomed from the hallway. Darcy, Elizabeth, and Anne bolted from their seats and exited toward the kitchen, escaping the parlour just a few seconds before the viscount breezed in to find his brother sipping tea amicably with Mrs. Collins and valiantly discussing the weather. They rose as he entered.

"Richard! What a surprise." The viscount eyed his brother warily as they exchanged short bows. "And Mrs. Collins!" He bowed to her curtsey. "It is early yet, for visiting. Yet I see that my brother is before me, so I shall not feel myself too indecorous."

"Indeed not, your Lordship," Mrs. Collins replied smoothly. "Will you have some tea?"

"I thank you, yes," he smiled, looking around expectantly.

Mrs. Collins and the colonel resumed their discussion, now taking up the subject of the villagers Mr. Collins had gone to call on. One had recently suffered the loss of his wife and newborn child. Another had been ill with a pox. Mrs. Collins, dutiful and well-informed about her husband's parish and all its concerns, was prepared to continue this line of conversation for some time, and the colonel, involved as he was in his annual review of Rosings' activities and ledgers, participated with unfeigned interest. But their conversation could not hold the viscount's attention for very long.

"Mrs. Collins." He spoke her name not as a question but as a command. She cast a regretful glance at the colonel before responding. "Yes, milord?"

"I was quite hoping to see Miss Bennet this morning. Is she about?"

"Milord, I am sorry I must say that she is not." Richard noted Mrs. Collins' neat evasion of an outright lie. "When the weather is fine she often rambles in the park for an hour or longer in the mornings."

"How long ago did she walk out?"

"I could not say exactly, milord."

Henry stood and made a show of looking out the window. "What an excellent idea. It is a beautiful morning. I shall also walk out. Perhaps I shall even be so fortunate as to encounter Miss Bennet in the park."

Richard could not resist poking at his brother. "Henry, what a fine thought. Shall I join you?"

"No!" Henry rounded on his brother with unveiled hostility, then quickly rearranged his expression into friendlier lines for the benefit of their hostess. "I meant, no, thank you, Richard, I will leave you to your tea and meet you later at the manor house." He bowed quickly and exited before either could rise or attempt to stop him.

Meanwhile, upstairs in Elizabeth's bedchamber, she and Anne sat on the bed as Darcy stood respectfully a few steps away, by the closed door. She had not been able to think of another safe place to take them as the viscount approached, so they had scurried as quietly as possible up the back stairs to the second floor.

Anne was still focused on her plan. "Elizabeth, please stand up."

Elizabeth stood obediently.

Anne continued. "Darcy, come over here please." He looked at his cousin questioningly but did as he was told, coming to face Elizabeth where she stood next to the bed. She looked up at him shyly as he took her hand and Anne spoke again.

"Now kiss her, Cousin."

"What?!" Elizabeth and Darcy gasped as if with one voice.

"'Tis very simple," Anne replied. "We cannot run the risk of Henry compromising her successfully so *you*, Cousin, shall compromise her first! And I shall be your witness." She beamed with self-satisfaction.

Every visible inch of Elizabeth was blushing pink. "I do not believe this is wise --"

"Sssshhhh," Darcy whispered, suddenly in perfect charity with his cousin. "Will you trust us, my love?" He placed his right index finger under her chin momentarily, and when she nodded, took her in his arms, leaned down, and applied his own lips to hers, gently at first, and then with more passion as she responded in kind. Anne averted her eyes briefly but could not resist a wistful peek. After a few seconds she decided that Elizabeth was sufficiently compromised that the embrace might cease.

She had not bargained on the passions of her cousin or her friend.

They continued to kiss, her hands behind his neck and entangled in his hair, his hands exploring her back and pulling her ever closer. Anne spoke their names once, then a second time, and then finally a third time, almost loudly enough to be heard in the parlour. Finally they separated slightly, Darcy resting his forehead upon Elizabeth's, both breathing heavily.

"Cousin Darcy!" Anne spoke sharply but with a twinkle in her eye. "You have well and thoroughly compromised Miss Elizabeth. What are your intentions?"

Darcy pulled Elizabeth closer and kissed the top of her head. "My intentions are most honourable. If she will have me, I shall secure a special licence and marry her as soon as may be."

"Very well," Anne replied. "Miss Elizabeth, do you accept Darcy's offer of marriage?"

Elizabeth looked up, smiling. "Yes, yes, I accept."

Anne nodded. "Good. It is now time for all three of us to leave for London. Elizabeth, how soon can you be packed?"

"I can certainly be ready in less than an hour."

"Excellent. Darcy, we shall return to Rosings, gather our things, and return to the parsonage with your carriage within that hour. But first come with me back to the parlour, in order that we may inform Richard and Mrs. Collins of these developments."

"Oh, my," giggled Elizabeth. "I had entirely forgotten about them."

"And who could blame you?" Anne was laughing also. "Darcy, you go first, just in case Henry is there. If he is not, then it will be safe for Elizabeth."

But no one was in the parlour when Darcy looked in, and so they betook themselves immediately to the manor house. Anne had already packed. Darcy took the stairs two at a time and pulled the cord for Perkins. There was no time to lose.

Three quarters of an hour later Perkins was directing Lady Catherine's footmen down the back stairs with Darcy's hastily packed trunks as well as his own, whilst Anne's traveling case was already strapped to the back of Darcy's carriage. Still there was no sign of Colonel Fitzwilliam and while neither Darcy nor Anne wished to depart without speaking with him, neither did they wish to tarry unnecessarily. Darcy sat briefly at his escritoire to scratch out a note to the colonel, but before he could finish it he heard the colonel's voice booming up the stairwell from the ground floor, whence the viscount's voice could also be heard, albeit somewhat more faintly, and from the sound of things it appeared that the colonel was not best pleased.

What is going on? Darcy hastened down the front stairs, first tossing the crumpled half-finished note into the fire.

In the drawing room, the Viscount Leicester wore a smug and complacent expression. Lady Catherine was looking aghast at her eldest nephew and his younger brother was glaring at him in open disapproval.

"Congratulate me, Darcy!" the viscount cried. "I am engaged to be married."

"If congratulations are in order, you shall certainly have them. To whom are you engaged?"

"To Miss Elizabeth Bennet!"

Darcy, steeled by months of concealing his innermost feelings, stepped forward with apparent complaisance. "Really, Henry? What a surprise! When did this happen?"

"Perhaps an hour and a quarter ago," he laughed self-consciously. "I encountered Miss Elizabeth on a walk in the park and my passions so overcame me that I embraced and kissed her. There were no witnesses, but despite Miss Elizabeth's maidenly resistance to the idea that she had been compromised, I impressed upon her that her reputation could be ruined if anyone ever found out, and that we must marry."

At this point Lady Catherine could contain herself no longer. "Henry, you owe this girl nothing. There were no witnesses. She used her arts and allurements to induce you to kiss her so that she could become a countess! Clearly she has even less shame than I imagined."

Richard slipped away to find Anne.

"So let me understand the timing, Cousin," Darcy said. "You said about an hour and a quarter ago?"

"Yes, give or take. I called on the parsonage and found Richard taking tea with Mrs. Collins. She said Miss Elizabeth had gone out for a walk so I went out into the park to search for her. Happily I found her very quickly, and once I did I was wholly unable to contain my ardour. She is quite compromised and we must marry."

"But if as you say there were no witnesses, how could anyone discover the incident? How can she be compromised if no one knows what happened?"

"Darcy! I am shocked to hear you say something so ungentlemanly. We all know now, of course, and naturally I informed my man Hopkins of my engagement upon my return to the house, so by now undoubtedly all the servants must be aware, and you know how they gossip..."

"In other words, you deliberately spread this story as widely as possible in an attempt to force Miss Elizabeth to marry you."

Henry had the good grace to look mildly sheepish. "You have caught me out, Cousin. Will you now wish me joy?"

"He will not." Anne had entered the room in time to hear most of the story.

"Anne! And why not?"

"Because despite everything you said, it is not true."

"What is not true?"

"You did not compromise Miss Elizabeth."

"Well, naturally she will deny it. I tried to allay her maidenly concerns but it seems I have not yet succeeded."

"No, Henry, you do not understand. Darcy and I know that you have not even seen Miss Elizabeth today, let alone compromised her."

"And how can you possibly believe that you could know that?"

"Because Darcy and I were with her this morning at the parsonage. Were we not, Richard?" She turned to her cousin with a nod.

"'Tis true, Henry, until the moment you arrived we had all been enjoying tea in the parlour with Mrs. Collins."

"And then she went out for her walk, where I met her."

"No, Henry." Anne's voice was cold. "When we heard your voice at the front door, Elizabeth and Darcy and I fled the parlour to avoid you. And would you like to know where we went?"

"You would like to tell me, I gather."

"We went to Miss Elizabeth's bedchamber."

"WHAT?!" Lady Catherine was shocked.

"And there," Anne continued, "after a few minutes, and at my suggestion, my cousin Darcy took Miss Elizabeth in his arms and kissed her thoroughly."

"NO!!" Lady Catherine bellowed.

"Yes, Mother, and I was their witness. It was not so very improper for Darcy to kiss her, since they were already engaged, but only one man in this room compromised Miss Elizabeth today, and it was not Cousin Henry."

"*ALREADY ENGAGED?!*" Lady Catherine was shouting even louder now. "But Anne! What of your prior claim on him? He must marry *you*!"

"Mother, how many times must I tell you that neither Darcy nor I desire such an outcome? I am very happy that he and Miss Elizabeth shall marry. They are good for each other."

"*Darcy!* What have you to say for yourself?" His aunt rounded on him. "Anne may have deluded herself into believing that she does not desire this match, but it was the favourite wish of both your mothers."

"*Enough*, Aunt Catherine. I have chosen my bride and she has accepted me. We will be married as soon as I can obtain her father's consent and a special licence."

In the excitement no one noticed at first that Henry Fitzwilliam had left the room. By the time they noticed, he had been gone for several minutes.

Chapter 17

Meanwhile, Elizabeth waited at the parsonage. Her trunks were packed and ready to be carried downstairs, but she remained in her bedchamber, watching out the window for the arrival of Darcy's carriage. It was with alarm and dread that instead she saw the Viscount Leicester on horseback, galloping into view.

She opened her door and hissed as loudly as she could, "Charlotte! CHARLOTTE!" but there was no reply. She wondered if Charlotte had left the house, and if the viscount was disposed toward forcing his way in, even if the maids told him that no one was home. But most of all she wondered when Darcy and Anne would come for her, and if it would be too late to avoid a scandal, and if the scandal would cause Darcy to rethink his desire to marry her. *I cannot be the cause of such a rift in his family. He would never want that. Blood is thicker than water, after all, and the viscount is his cousin, and is the colonel's BROTHER! They cannot take my side against him. How could they?*

The knocker sounded, heavy and hard. Leaning out her open chamber door, Elizabeth heard feet scurrying toward the front door. The maid, Sally, was answering. Yes, the mistress was at home to His Lordship. Elizabeth released the breath she had been holding, knowing that Charlotte would not give her up, and closed her door soundlessly, hoping to see Darcy's carriage when she looked out the window. But no conveyances were yet visible.

Unable to resist the temptation, she silently cracked open her door again to hear what she could. His Lordship seemed little able to modulate his voice, and while she could not make out Charlotte's words, she could certainly get the gist of their conversation from hearing his end of it.

"Mrs. Collins! How can Elizabeth have gone out for another walk so soon? She had a long walk just an hour ago!"

"I have every right to use her Christian name. We have just become engaged."

"I am a man of honour, and although I was overcome by my ardour in the park, my intentions are honourable and I shall marry Elizabeth as soon as possible. In fact, she and I shall be departing for Matlock House in London this afternoon, so that I may present her to my parents as my future bride."

Elizabeth, listening upstairs, could only think, *I must stay as far away from him and his carriage as possible.*

"Yes, undoubtedly. I am quite certain that she has accepted me, although obviously she had no choice, once she was compromised."

"Mrs. Collins, I am becoming suspicious. Are you quite

certain that Elizabeth is not in the house?"

"I am sure you could have no objection to providing me with a tour of the house, Mrs. Collins. I know my aunt has made many improvements since my last visit, and I should very much like to see them."

Elizabeth heard these words with unalloyed dread. Not waiting for His Lordship's next utterance, she slipped out of her room. Where to hide? She remembered an enormous linen airing cupboard in the hall, near the back stairs, and knew that there would be room for her there. Hearing steps on the stairs, she opened the door of that closet and entered it, pulling the door closed behind her silently, and stepping behind a drying rack laden with freshly laundered bedsheets and a large shelf of folded towels for concealment in the event someone opened the door. The lint tickled her nose. It was not the best plan, but it was all she had, and as she settled herself inside, she gave thanks that even as a child she had never been afraid of the dark.

The steps were louder now, ascending. Charlotte's voice was louder too; as they reached the upstairs hall and began the "tour," she welcomed the viscount to each chamber in turn, hoping Elizabeth would hear her and keep far away. "Your Lordship, here is Mr. Collins' bedchamber, and here next to it is my own." Doors were opened and Elizabeth could hear the viscount's boots stomping around each room. She wondered idly if he was peering under all the beds and looking into the closets. HAH! When he looked into hers, he would see only the shelves that Lady Catherine had had installed.

"...And here is Maria's bedchamber, and here is Miss Elizabeth's bedchamber." Elizabeth could hear the stress in Charlotte's voice as she opened the door to Elizabeth's room and the relief as she observed to him that, as he could see, it was empty. She heard him go in and look around, open and close the closet door. Next came a faint thud.

"Her trunks are packed! What is she about?"

"Did not your Lordship just say that the two of you were planning to depart for London this afternoon?"

"Yes. I shall send my carriage and footmen to collect her belongings straight away so that we may be off as soon as she returns from her walk."

They returned in the direction whence they had come, until they sounded as if they were standing immediately outside the linen closet where Elizabeth had taken refuge.

"And what is this door here, Mrs. Collins?"

"It is the linen closet, milord."

"Will you show it to me?"

Charlotte opened the closet door. The drying rack covered with sheets stood front and center. Piles of sheets and towels were visible on shelves inside, the pale muslin of Elizabeth's gown neatly camouflaged behind them; she held her breath. He leaned over and peered into the dimness, then straightened, seemingly satisfied.

Charlotte closed the closet door.

And then Elizabeth sneezed.

The sneeze echoed through the closet and she did not dare hope that it had been inaudible to those on the other side of the door.

The viscount roared and pulled the door open again, but Elizabeth was ready. She pulled a large still-damp bedsheet off the drying rack and as he charged toward her, she threw it over his head and upper body. As he struggled with it, she followed with a second sheet, wrapping the corners around him until he was hopelessly entangled, and then on her way out of the closet pulled the drying rack down behind her, where it landed on the floor between the swaddled viscount and the door. Slamming the door from the outside, she looked at Charlotte with the wild exhilaration of one who has survived a terrifying experience.

"Is there any heavy piece of furniture we can move in front of the closet door?"

"Better yet," said Charlotte, brandishing a key from her chatelaine, and turning it in the lock. This was not a moment too soon, as they heard the drying rack crash against the door, and then the viscount trying the knob and pounding from the inside, demanding to be released.

***

As Colonel Fitzwilliam came running toward the parsonage, his cousin Darcy close behind, he noticed his brother's horse tied up at one side of the house, and knowing that time was of the essence, let himself in the unlocked front door and hastened to the parlour. Finding it empty, but hearing voices and heavy footfalls upstairs, he hurried up the stairs, only to find a sight he had not expected. Elizabeth Bennet and Charlotte Collins were sitting on the floor in the hallway, leaning against a door. They were in near hysterics of laughter, with tears streaming down their faces. And someone – was that *Henry?!* – was pounding on the door from the other side, shouting to be released.

"Ladies?" The colonel looked from one to the other.

Charlotte and Elizabeth looked up at him, fully intending to respond, only to realise that they could not stop laughing.

There was more pounding on the closet door. "LET ME OUT!" Yes, it was definitely the viscount. Mrs. Collins held up a key from her chatelaine and waggled it at Elizabeth and the colonel, and the ladies continued to laugh. The colonel could not resist a chuckle of his own as he contemplated this scene, then more than a chuckle, and by the time Darcy found them a few seconds later, all three were laughing uproariously. He looked from Elizabeth to Charlotte to the colonel, and when he heard his other cousin shouting from inside the closet, and saw the key in Charlotte's hand, even sober Darcy could not resist the temptation to join the others in mirth.

After they had all caught their breath a little, Darcy stepped over to extend his hands to Charlotte and Elizabeth to help them up from the floor. When both ladies were safely restored to vertical postures he took Elizabeth in his arms, and as she finally felt and knew that now she was safe, she was struck by the enormity of the danger she had evaded, and before she knew it she was sobbing with relief. He stroked her hair and handed her his handkerchief as Charlotte and the colonel looked on in sympathy.

"LET ME OUT OF HERE, WOMAN!" Henry's voice boomed. "I WILL NOT TOLERATE SUCH BEHAVIOUR! YOU WILL BE AN OBEDIENT WIFE!" Elizabeth shuddered in Darcy's arms and he pulled her closer.

Darcy glanced at the colonel, then at the closet door. "What shall we do with him, Richard? I do not feel he is ready to be released just yet."

Charlotte spoke up. "It would be unwise to release him. He expressed a plan to load Elizabeth and her possessions into his carriage this afternoon and head to London."

Darcy and the colonel looked at each other and nodded. The colonel spoke first.

"Thank you, Mrs. Collins. Darcy, here is my suggestion. Resume your plan. Finish packing your carriage and go, the two of you and Anne, to London. After you have been gone an hour or so, it will be reasonable for Mrs. Collins to release Henry from his gaol. Until then, I fear what he will do if he is able to get out."

The viscount was able to discern his brother's voice outside the door. "Richard! Brother! Surely the vixen will hear reason from YOU and let me out!"

"Nay, Henry, if anyone in this house needs to hear reason, it is you."

"Then LET ME OUT so I may hear it!"

"Not just yet, Henry."

The colonel spoke quietly to Mrs. Collins, who relinquished the closet key to his keeping and then directed him to the writing desk in her sitting room. Shaking an amused finger at Darcy and Elizabeth, she separated them gently and directed them to the parlour, calling to Sally to bring tea to that room.

"I SHOULD LIKE SOME TEA IN THE PARLOUR," the viscount shouted.

She ignored him and repaired to that room herself. As she arrived there, so, from the other direction, did Colonel Fitzwilliam, having written a hasty note to his father the Earl, at his house in Town. "I am off to find an express rider," he advised. "I shall be back within the hour, Mrs. Collins," he added, waving the closet door key, "but my father must be made aware of what has transpired here. Henry wrote to me of his intentions and so I will be able to provide sufficient evidence that Father should believe me. He would never have approved of Henry's plan to secure a wife by dishonouring her."

Darcy agreed. "My uncle will be appalled, but he needs to know; you are doing as you must. And if you see Anne, please ask her to come to the parsonage with my carriage and footmen. We shall load Elizabeth's trunks and then we shall be off. We shall stop just long enough in London to acquire a special licence and send a note to Bingley apprising him of our imminent arrival, and then we shall make for Hertfordshire, where I shall seek a private interview with Mr. Bennet as soon as possible." He squeezed Elizabeth's hand and smiled down at her.

From the entrance hall was now heard a voice that could not have been welcome to any of those present. Mr. Collins had returned home, and he was displeased, for Lady Catherine had acquainted him with her views about the morning's events, and he viewed it as his moral duty as Her Ladyship's parson to support and reinforce her opinions in all matters relating to her family, the parish, household matters, gardening, the care of livestock, and any other subjects in which she might express an interest, but especially the marital disposition of her only child.

So when he entered the parlour – his own parlour – only to find his sly adventuress of a cousin seated entirely too close to Lady Catherine's distinguished nephew on a settee, and his wife calmly serving tea to them, he could not be silent. He bowed sullenly to Colonel Fitzwilliam as the colonel took his leave and then rounded on Elizabeth.

"Cousin! You must leave this place at once! Lady Catherine is quite out of sympathy with the way you have used your arts and allurements to seduce her nephew, who is promised to her daughter Anne! How could you comport yourself in such a godless way? Have you no shame at all?! No shame?! I shall write to your father and inform him of your actions."

Darcy stood and raised himself to his full height, more than a head taller than the parson, his patience exhausted. "Mr. Collins! You will do no such thing. Miss Elizabeth is betrothed to me. My cousin and I have no understanding, nor has either of us ever desired one. Desist now from your threats or I shall be forced to have a word with my godfather the archbishop about your suitability for the Lord's work."

The parson was not so easily turned aside. Bowing deeply, he replied, "But Mr. Darcy, sir, with all respect to you, sir, Lady Catherine was quite explicit in her account of your betrothal to Miss de Bourgh."

Miss de Bourgh herself corrected him, having entered

without being announced. "No, Mr. Collins. No. I am not engaged to my cousin. No, I have no desire to marry him, just as he has no desire to marry me. My mother is suffering from a delusion."

Mr. Collins was briefly speechless. But only briefly. "Miss de Bourgh, you are confused. Your mother has assured me --"

Darcy had reached the limits of his forbearance. "Mr. Collins, be silent, and speak not of things you know not." Heavy footsteps were audible now on the back stairs. Anne explained, "The footmen are bringing down Elizabeth's trunks. We can be off in a moment, Darcy, if the two of you are ready."

Collins stepped forward as if to block Elizabeth's exit. "I cannot permit this, Cousin."

Not stepping back, Elizabeth advanced on him. "Did you not admonish me, just five minutes ago, that I must leave Hunsford, that you were casting me out? My dear Mr. Collins, I am simply obeying your instructions." She smiled sweetly, turned to her betrothed, and said, "Yes, let us be off." He made a show of kissing her hand, which agitated the parson further. Elizabeth stepped over to give Charlotte a heartfelt embrace, with whispered promises of future correspondence, and the three walked out to Darcy's fully loaded equipage. He handed the ladies in, climbed in himself, and with a gentle jolt the carriage was off toward the London road.

Mr. Collins turned on his wife. "Mrs. Collins! You will immediately sever your acquaintance with my immoral cousin! She shall never be welcome under my roof again."

"Mr. Collins, I think it is very unlikely that the future Mrs. Darcy would ever seek accommodation under your roof."

"She will not be -- " he stopped for a moment, having become aware of a faint pounding and shouting that sounded as if it were coming from upstairs. "Mrs. Collins, is someone upstairs in the house?"

"The Viscount Leicester is upstairs, Mr. Collins."

"What is he doing up there, and why is he making so much noise?"

"He is locked in the linen airing cupboard, Mr. Collins."

Mr. Collins, not generally noted for his lithe movements, burst out of the parlour and raced up the stairs. The viscount's pounding was sporadic, punctuated with shouts and threats about what he would do to those who had so entrapped him, not considering that such threats did not make the prospect of his release very appealing to those involved.

The parson advanced upon the locked closet door and bowed deeply. Charlotte, a few steps behind, covered her mouth to keep from laughing.

"Viscount Leicester! We are honored to receive you in our home."

"ARE YOU MAD, MR. COLLINS?! LET ME OUT!"

"Of course, your lordship. Mrs. Collins, you will release the viscount at once."

"I am sorry to tell you, Mr. Collins, that it is quite

impossible."

"How can it be impossible?"

"I do not have the key."

He gestured at her chatelaine of perhaps a dozen keys. "And what are those?"

"These are other keys."

"But I have seen you open this closet many times before."

"I did not say I had never had the key, only that I do not have it now."

"Who has it, then?"

"The viscount's brother, Colonel Fitzwilliam, has the key at present."

"How did he get it?"

"I gave it to him."

"When did you give it to him?"

"A few minutes after I locked the viscount in the closet."

"Mrs. Collins, why did you lock the viscount in the closet?!"

"Because he was attempting to abduct Elizabeth."

The viscount bellowed, "SHE IS MY BETROTHED! SHE WILL BE MY WIFE! IT IS HER DUTY TO OBEY ME! I

CANNOT BE SAID TO ABDUCT HER!"

Mr. Collins looked at Charlotte in astonishment. "My cousin's arts and allurements are potent indeed, if she has engaged herself to two men of noble descent in as many days. It is good that she has gone."

"GONE?!" the viscount shouted. 'WHERE HAS SHE GONE? WITHOUT A FAREWELL TO HER BETROTHED?"

Charlotte was out of patience. "Your Lordship, she is not your betrothed. My friend has accepted a proposal of marriage from your cousin Darcy, and they are off to London with your cousin Anne as chaperone."

Mr. Collins began to interrupt, but she raised a hand in his direction, and something in her look kept him silent. She continued, "Your brother now holds the key to this closet. He asked for the key and I gave it to him to ensure that you would not be able to escape in time to interfere with your cousin's plan."

"WHERE IS MY BROTHER NOW? WHEN WILL HE RETURN?!"

Charlotte did not feel it was her place to inform the viscount that his brother had written to their father to disclose the viscount's unsavoury behaviour. "He had an urgent errand in the village. He should be back within the hour."

"ANOTHER HOUR?!"

"I cannot say, your Lordship. I do not know exactly when he will return, or whether he will release you immediately when he does. When he does return I will make his presence known to you. It is now time for me to return to the parlour."

She turned and walked away, then down the stairs. Her husband followed, glaring after her darkly, but then, eager to make himself useful to his patroness, was off immediately to acquaint Her Ladyship with the newest turn of events.

Charlotte returned to the parlour and picked up a biscuit, only to hear the continuing faint pounding and shouting of "LET ME OUT!" With a sigh, she decided that the garden would be more pleasant than remaining indoors. She took up a book and headed for her favourite bench overlooking the rhododendrons, where Colonel Fitzwilliam found her a half hour later.

"Oh, Mrs. Collins. What a day it has been."

"You must be exhausted, Colonel. I can offer tea and sandwiches if you are in need of sustenance."

"What a capital idea. I shall take you up on it."

"Shall we return to the house, then?"

"Yes." His face fell. "It is time I released Henry from his captivity. He will be very unhappy."

"He asked me where you were. I did not disclose to him that you were sending an express to the Earl."

"He will know that soon enough. I shall have to tell him." The colonel slapped a fence post in frustration. "I do not know what has come over him! To believe that he could take advantage of a gentlewoman so shamefully, as a privilege of his rank! I could never have imagined that he had become capable of such a thing. And then to lie about it! If he had actually compromised her deliberately, that would be bad enough – the act of a rake. But to spin a lie about having compromised a woman he had not even seen today – that was beyond anything, Mrs. Collins."

***

"LET ME OUT!"

"Henry, are you still in there?"

"RICHARD! FATHER WILL BE MOST DISPLEASED!"

"I agree; he will. Especially once he learns that you plotted to ruin a young woman for your own selfish purposes."

"RUIN HER?! I WOULD HAVE MADE HER A COUNTESS!"

"Against her will."

"SHE WOULD HAVE GOT OVER IT QUICKLY ENOUGH WHEN SHE GOT HER PIN MONEY."

"Henry. I am going to unlock the door in a moment. But I need your word of honour that you will not attempt to escape. Darcy and Miss Elizabeth are long gone; you cannot catch them. You must acknowledge that your plan has failed. Do I have your word?"

"DO NOT BE MELODRAMATIC, RICHARD."

"That is not an answer to my question. Do I have your

word that you will not pursue Miss Elizabeth further?"

There was a pause.

"OF COURSE, RICHARD, WHAT DO YOU TAKE ME FOR?"

The colonel stepped forward with the key and turned it in the lock. "Very well, Henry. You may come out now."

Henry Fitzwilliam, the Viscount Leicester, somewhat the worse for wear and covered with lint, emerged into the light of day and stepped into his brother's arms. The colonel patted his brother on the back gently, then released him slowly. He had never seen his bluff, confident elder brother looking so utterly defeated, even hopeless, his eyes hollow. It was a sight he would never forget.

"Henry. I am sorry. But it was quite impossible for us to allow your plan to succeed."

"She loves Darcy? She truly loves him? And he loves her?"

"Yes. They love each other very much."

"Then I wish them joy. But I am in a bad spot, Richard, and I know not what I shall do."

"There is no need to decide that now. Would you care for some tea and sandwiches, Henry? You must be hungry and thirsty."

"Yes, thank you, after I refresh myself. Give me a minute."

Mrs. Collins curtsied and hastened to ask Sally to bring

more tea. The colonel met her in the parlour, where they waited for the viscount in a companionable silence, lest he overhear any conversation they might have.

When he did not appear after a few minutes, they began to wonder if he had broken his word. Then they heard the sound of a gunshot through the windows, and with a sense of dread the colonel bolted from the house and ran in the direction from which the sound had come. Perhaps a hundred yards from the house he discovered the body of his brother, his pistol by his side, a bullet through his head. Dropping to his knees, he took the lifeless viscount in his arms and wept.

"Oh, Henry! What became of you? Was it really so bad? How did you become capable of such cruelty and violence?"

Charlotte, a few steps behind, could only gasp when she reached the scene. Withdrawing to the house, she quietly requested a cart be brought to the colonel's location.

The next few hours were a blur of activity. Charlotte sent a servant to Rosings with a note acquainting Lady Catherine with the fate of her eldest nephew. The colonel wrote letters to his father and to Darcy, to inform them of the horrific development, and Charlotte arranged for them to be sent via express rider. Meanwhile, Mr. Collins returned to the parsonage and condoled the bereaved brother until he was forced to retreat to Rosings for peace and quiet, a purpose for which Richard Fitzwilliam had never previously sought his aunt's home. The magistrate was summoned and quickly rendered a finding of death by misadventure. There was, after all, no need for a scandal.

Soaking in a restorative hot bath before bed that evening,

the colonel reflected on the events of the day. He had loved his brother but could find it in his heart to be glad for Darcy's sake, as well as Miss Elizabeth's, that Henry's threat to their felicity existed no longer. He was grateful to Anne for her role in helping the couple evade Henry's designs and escape the neighbourhood. He wondered how Anne's relationship with her mother would be altered by this streak of independence and rebellion he had observed. And, face in his hands as his batman poured the hot water over his hair, he allowed himself to reflect on the ways in which his own life was about to change more than anyone's.

He was utterly spent, so a single short glass of brandy enabled him to find sleep quickly.

Chapter 18

Darcy, Elizabeth, Anne, and Georgiana were at the dinner table at Darcy House when the express arrived. A footman brought it in on a silver tray and presented it to his master, advising that no immediate reply was needed. Darcy tore the note open immediately, scanning quickly as the others waited for the news. When he glanced up he saw that they were all looking at him worriedly.

"It is from Richard," he said. "Henry is dead, by his own hand." Elizabeth gasped. Georgiana whimpered faintly.

Elizabeth reached over and took his hand. "I am so sorry. I know you cared for your cousin."

Darcy leaned back in his chair and rubbed his eyes. "I did care for Henry. We played together as children, and I loved him like a brother in those days, although later I became closer to Richard. But I did not recognize the man he became, at the end. I do not know what to make of all this. What a dreadful waste."

He took a shuddering breath, pulled out his handkerchief, and dabbed at his eyes as the women looked on. After a few moments he looked up at Elizabeth. "I would be untruthful if I did not say that in a terrible way this is a relief, knowing that his designs on you are at an end, my love."

Elizabeth was inclined to be generous, now that the viscount's threats were in the past. "We can only wonder what extremity of circumstances caused him to behave as he did, these last few days."

"I know what the circumstances were," Anne said. "Or at least part of them. Henry owed very substantial gambling debts. I overheard him speaking with his valet about them. I mean many thousands of pounds, and he was apparently being pressed for payment."

"He was a future earl! No gentleman would have pressed him for payment," said Darcy.

"These debts were not owed to *gentlemen*," Anne replied.

"Oh," Elizabeth said, shocked.

Darcy nodded. "Yes, Richard had heard something of this from a friend a few days ago."

Anne continued, "He had had significant debts of honour, and in order to retire them he had availed himself of the services of a moneylender, who was pressing him aggressively. He needed to get money from the Earl, but the Earl was demanding that he settle down and marry, and had given him an ultimatum to find a wife by the first of May, or lose his financial support."

Elizabeth nodded. "This explains so much! I could not understand his urgency."

"And now he is gone." Georgiana was still shocked by all she had heard. "Poor dear Henry! If only he had let his family know about his troubles, I am sure someone could have helped him. Would you not have helped him, brother?"

"I have given Henry money several times in the past few years, Georgie. I no longer accounted for these transactions as loans, for I knew it was quite unlikely he would ever repay me. Had he asked again, to be frank with you, sweetling, I know not what I would have said."

"Ohhhh." Her lower lip was trembling and Elizabeth was up out of her seat immediately, with her arm around her future sister's shoulders. "I know it is very hard to hear these things, but please do not upset yourself too much. Your cousin was a fundamentally good person who had a bad problem and did not know how else to try to solve it." She wrapped the teenager in a warm hug, which was quickly reciprocated. Darcy looked across the table at the two women he loved most in the world, embracing each other for comfort and solace, and allowed himself a quiet smile of relief. *Yes. I knew it could be like this.*

Anne, looking from him to the sweet tableau across and back, enjoyed a tiny but satisfied smile of her own.

No one had much of an appetite any longer, but the party was still at table when the Earl of Matlock was announced. They all rose to greet him. He was impeccably dressed, as always, but his eyes were rimmed in red and his hair was wild, as if he had been raking it with his fingers. He moved to his nephew and enfolded him in his arms, trembling with emotion.

"Darcy."

"Uncle."

They stood there for a long moment until breaking apart and acknowledging the others. "Uncle, may I present Miss Elizabeth Bennet of Longbourn in Hertfordshire, who has agreed to be my wife?"

The Earl stepped over to Elizabeth, who curtseyed deeply to him, and looked her up and down. "So you are the young lady who – my son wrote to me of you. Both my sons, actually. I am very pleased to make your acquaintance, Miss Bennet." She blushed fiercely as he kissed her hand, then turned to his nieces and embraced each in turn. A footman brought a chair and a place setting to table for him.

"Uncle, will you eat?"

"I will try, Darcy. It is good to be with others at such a time. I had given Henry a – " He began to break down. "I had given Henry an ultimatum. To find a wife and return to London, or lose my financial support." Placing his elbows on the table, he rested his head upon his hands and shuddered with grief. Anne, seated next to him, placed her arm around his shoulders protectively. After a few seconds he sat upright again and took her hand in his before trying to speak again.

"I am sorry to be so emotional."

"Uncle! You have lost your son and heir. Of course you are distressed. We are your family and you may indulge in front of us in any way you need to."

He looked around the room. "Yes. You are all my family, including you, Miss Elizabeth. I always wondered what kind of paragon of womanhood it would take to win my nephew's heart, not to mention his approval, and I know from my sons' reports that he has chosen well."

Elizabeth was touched. "Thank you, sir."

The Earl took a few bites. The others did the same, for politeness' sake. The Earl inquired after Anne's health and commended her on how well she looked, asked after Georgiana's lessons, and then, wishing to know more about Elizabeth, engaged her in exclusive conversation for a few minutes. The others looked on as they chatted. Even Darcy, as much as he already admired her ease in company, was impressed by the way she maintained a balance between respecting the Earl and still treating him as her equal, and it was clear that the Earl himself found her manners entirely satisfactory.

The Earl turned to his host. "I must depart for Matlock tomorrow, Darcy. We need to make arrangements −" His voice broke, he said no more, and Darcy understood. "When will you be able to join us?"

"My plan has been to travel to Hertfordshire tomorrow, sir, to ask Mr. Bennet for his blessing for our marriage."

"Oh, yes, by all means, you must do that."

"I had planned on a more extended stay in Hertfordshire at the home of my friend Bingley, but ..." He looked at Elizabeth, who nodded. "...under the circumstances I think it best for me to join you and the rest of the family in Matlock as soon thereafter as possible."

"Brother?" Georgiana's eyes had lit up. "Might Anne and I remain in Hertfordshire after you leave? I know we would both enjoy spending time with Elizabeth and meeting her family."

At the thought of Elizabeth's family and their friendship with Wickham, Darcy grimaced involuntarily. Pausing to decide what to say, he caught Elizabeth's eye again, and she spoke, putting her hand on Georgiana's. "That sounds like a lovely idea, but let us allow your brother to make his plans first, and then we can discuss the rest of it later." She nodded at him almost imperceptibly and Darcy almost wept with relief. *She has handled it. She will handle it. She is a marvel. And she will be mine.* The thought of the life he could look forward to would see him through the difficult days and weeks ahead.

Georgiana stood and led Anne and Elizabeth to the door. "Will we see you in a few minutes, Brother? And you also, Uncle?"

Both agreed, and the ladies went through to the drawing room.

Darcy poured port for himself and his uncle.

"Richard must resign his commission at once. He is now my heir and I cannot allow him to return to the Continent."

"I am certain he will understand that, sir."

"And I will not give him any ultimatums, but he needs to find a wife. Do I understand that Miss Bennet has four sisters?"

Darcy almost choked on his port, and coughed vigorously for a few seconds while the Earl slapped him on the back. "Sir, I —"

"Never mind, son, I was only sporting with you."

Thank God for that. "Did Richard tell you his immediate plans, sir?"

"He will depart at first light to transport Henry back to Matlock. We will plan the services but will delay them until you can be with us."

"That is very good of you, sir. I esteemed Henry greatly, and despite these last few days, I will always remember him with great fondness."

"Now let us rejoin the ladies, Darcy. I am sure one of them is missing you very badly."

When they walked into the drawing room Elizabeth was in close conversation with Georgiana, with Anne looking on. Georgiana was nodding her head but looked a little pale. The gentlemen sat down and Georgiana rang for tea and coffee. Darcy was proud of his sister, acting as his gracious hostess under such bizarre conditions. He could see more and more of their mother in her every day. She would be a great lady.

After she had poured out the tea and coffee, she said quietly to her brother, "Elizabeth has informed me of the presence of ... a certain person ... in Hertfordshire. Is that why you made a face when I said I might like to stay in the neighbourhood for a little while?"

"Yes, poppet. I did not want him to intrude upon your

notice again, especially at a time when I cannot be there with you."

"Very well, I shall remain here for now, but when you are able to return to Hertfordshire, I would like to go with you, and for us both to make a stay, whether he is there or not."

"And so you shall." He kissed her forehead.

Chapter 19

In the morning, having sent word to Bingley the day before, Darcy handed Anne and Elizabeth into the Darcy carriage and departed for Hertfordshire. By early afternoon they were pulling up in front of Netherfield. Refreshed and settled in the drawing room, they began to acquaint their host with recent events, rendering their normally garrulous and ebullient friend as speechless and silent as Darcy had ever seen him.

But only for a moment. This was Charles Bingley, after all.

"How shocking. What a terrible fate for the viscount and for his family."

"Yes, it has been quite a blow to my uncle."

Bingley was quiet for a moment, then looked up with a grin. "But Darcy! You have been a dark horse indeed! Engaged to Miss Elizabeth! We are to be brothers! Congratulations! I should never have imagined it. I cannot wait to inform Caroline. Or, better yet, perhaps I should just allow her to read the notice in the papers. Miss Elizabeth, may I offer my best wishes? This stubborn mule of a friend does have many fine qualities, and I daresay you will discover them all soon enough."

Elizabeth laughed. "We are not officially engaged yet. Shortly I must return to Longbourn, and Mr. Darcy shall have the unenviable task of soliciting my hand from my father."

"How did it go for you, Bingley?" Darcy was understandably curious, and perhaps somewhat wary. "Did Bennet give you a hard time?"

"Yes, he did, a little. He reminded me of the way I had injured Jane by leaving the neighbourhood so suddenly without returning or sending word, and demanded my solemn promise that I would treat her with all consideration in future." Darcy swallowed hard, reminded of his complicity in Bingley's behaviour.

Bingley brightened. "But then he shook my hand and said that since Jane loved me and had chosen me he could not gainsay her."

Darcy was not looking forward to his encounter with Mr. Bennet but knew no good could come of delaying it further. Looking over at his intended, he asked, "Shall we be off to Longbourn?" Elizabeth's trunks were still on the back of his carriage so all that was necessary was for the ladies to don their bonnets and cloaks to be handed in again for the three-mile ride. Elizabeth had sent her father a note from London the day before but did not know whether it had yet arrived, and thus whether they were expected.

Longbourn was quiet when they arrived. Mrs. Bennet and her youngest two daughters had gone to call on Aunt

Phillips, and Mary was reading somewhere out in the back garden, but Jane was there to welcome Elizabeth with open arms, and to accept an introduction to Anne, as well as everyone's congratulations on her engagement. Elizabeth, eager to see her father, was still in her cloak when she knocked on the door of his book room.

"Lizzy! I just received your note! Is all well with you, my dear?" He gave her a warm embrace.

"Yes, papa, all is very well."

"I am sorry your mother and sisters are not all here to give you the noisy greeting I am sure you were hoping for." He winked at her and they both laughed.

"Come out to the parlour, papa. There is someone I would like you to meet." Taking him by the hand, she led him to the sitting room where Jane was talking with Darcy and Anne. "Papa, I would like to present Miss Anne de Bourgh. Anne is the daughter of Lady Catherine de Bourgh. And you will remember Mr. Darcy. They have been kind enough to bring me home."

"Shall I ask Hill for tea, father?" Jane inquired.

"Yes, my dear, let us all have some tea."

Darcy cleared his throat. "Sir, before the tea is brought, may I beg a few moments of your time?"

Mr. Bennet looked at Darcy searchingly just in time to observe a very interesting exchange of glances between his guest and his second daughter. He sighed and stood, "Yes, by all means, Mr. Darcy. Let us go to my book room." He regarded that daughter with apprehension. "Lizzy, you look as though you would very much like to join us." Confirming his suspicions, she blushed to the tips of her ears, but she stood and followed him toward the library, Darcy trailing behind. Jane remained behind with Anne, who could not conceal her wide grin, and turned to her for information.

As soon as Mr. Bennet was settled behind his desk, Darcy spoke. "Sir, I have come to ask for Miss Elizabeth Bennet's hand in marriage." She reached over and squeezed his hand, a gesture not lost on her father. Darcy continued, "I hold her in the most tender regard, and it would be my honour to care for her for the rest of our lives."

He reached into his pocket and drew out a folded document. "Here is a draft of the settlement I propose to make on her, for your review and approval." He placed it in his future father's hand.

"Mr. Darcy, please allow me a few minutes of complete surprise. When last I saw you it seemed you considered my daughter tolerable, but not handsome enough to tempt you. This seems quite a turnabout. Perhaps you could enlighten me. What exactly has happened to bring the two of you to this point?"

Darcy and Elizabeth smiled at one another and she squeezed his hand again. The younger man took a deep breath. "Very well, sir. It is quite a tale …."

***

In the parlour, Jane was listening to Anne's rendition of the story in near disbelief. "You stabbed her thumb with an *embroidery needle?!*"

"It was the only way I could think of to keep her from being obligated to go to the pianoforte, Miss Bennet."

"Please, call me Jane."

"Then you must call me Anne. I could not let Henry carry out a scheme of such wickedness, especially knowing that Darcy and Elizabeth loved each other." Anne sipped her tea and nibbled on a biscuit. "Darcy's sister Georgiana was unable to make this trip with us, but she is very much looking forward to having Elizabeth as her sister."

Jane nodded vigorously. "Miss Darcy is very lucky. I am delighted to be marrying Mr. Bingley, but I shall miss Lizzy so much. She is the most loyal, caring, wonderful sister I can imagine." She glanced toward her father's book room. "I only wish I could hear my father's reaction to the story of their courtship. How dramatic it sounds, especially the last few days!"

"Trust me, Jane, I have not done it justice."

They enjoyed their tea for a few more minutes until they heard the library door open, and footsteps in the hall. When Mr. Bennet led the affianced couple into the parlour Anne and Jane were already standing to greet them.

"This will not come as a surprise to anyone, but Mr. Darcy has requested Elizabeth's hand, and been accepted, and I have given them my blessing."

Congratulations ensued all around. Jane called for more tea and the rest of the afternoon passed delightfully at Longbourn.

***

Much could be said (but need not be) of the joyous exclamations of Mrs. Bennet upon learning of her second daughter's brilliant match. Luckily for Darcy, that worthy lady was not informed until the following morning, so the most extreme effusions occurred whilst he was already on the road to Matlock, where he would assist his uncle, aunt, and cousin in addressing the aftermath of the viscount's death.

By the time he returned with Georgiana and Anne, all Mrs. Bennet's former dislike thrown over and forgotten, she had tempered her enthusiasm sufficiently that she could focus on learning his favourite dishes and other preferences in order to cater to him in every way. He in turn learned to accept her attentions and various eccentricities with grace, by remembering that despite her many shortcomings she was, after all, the woman who had delivered his beloved, and by spending as many peaceful hours with his future father-in-law as he could, whilst his bride-to-be passed many happy afternoons with his sister and cousin as her own escape. By spending time together, all learned to love one another even more.

With mourning for the viscount already one month complete, it was agreed that a double wedding with Jane and Bingley in two months' time would be just the thing, and in short order the happy event was scheduled. Darcy, Anne, and Georgiana, along with Bingley, were daily visitors at Longbourn, and the happy summer weather meant plenty of time spent walking outdoors, in the gardens, and even enjoying the occasional picnic. But one day they were all seated in the parlour (save Mr. Bennet, ensconced in his book room playing chess with Darcy, and Mrs. Bennet, calling on her sister with her two youngest daughters) when an ornate carriage pulled into the drive and disgorged Lady Catherine and Mr. Collins. When they were announced Elizabeth cast a wary eye at Anne, who nodded back at her with a steeliness in her gaze Elizabeth had never seen before.

The parson spoke first. "Cousin Elizabeth! You must desist from this foolish - "

"Be silent, Mr. Collins! I will speak to your cousin, who has used her arts and allurements so shamelessly to entrap my nephew! This engagement shall not stand."

"Hello, Mother." Anne stepped forward.

"Anne! How can you stand by and allow this social climber to take your rightful place by Darcy's side?"

"Elizabeth Bennet is a lady in every way, Mother, and most importantly, she is a lady who loves my cousin Darcy, and whom Darcy loves in turn. They shall be wed because they belong together."

"Anne! Have you been reading novels? That is not how life works. Your joining with your cousin will unite two great estates."

"Mother. I do not wish to marry Darcy, and he does not wish to marry me. We do not wish to unite our estates. We are both infinitely happier under the present arrangement. I cannot understand why you would travel all the way to Hertfordshire to carry on this way. I told you in Kent what my feelings were, and they are unchanged."

"Anne! My child, what are feelings when compared to your duty?! Think of the future of our family! Are the shades of Pemberley to be polluted by this tawdry adventuress? Are her paltry bloodlines to be mixed with the noble line of Fitzwilliam and the distinguished line of Darcy? Is this lowborn chit to hold herself out as the niece of an earl, and your cousin, and Georgiana's sister? Is she to pretend to be my niece? It is not to be borne!" She turned to Elizabeth and snarled, "Is it money you want? I will offer you fifty thousand pounds to desist from your pursuit of my nephew." She opened her reticule and pulled out an enormous sheaf of banknotes.

Mr. Collins looked as if he were about to faint, but rallied quickly and interjected, "Cousin Elizabeth, with such a sum you could care for your family when - "

"No, Mr. Collins. This discussion does not concern you." Elizabeth glared at her cousin and turned to Lady Catherine, her tone flat and unemotional.

"Lady Catherine, let us now come to a right understanding. Your nephew is a gentleman, and I am a gentleman's daughter. So far we are equal. Both he and Anne have stated repeatedly that they are not bound to one another by honour or affection beyond the usual cousinly regard. If they are not bound by your preferences, then why should I, a person wholly unconnected with you, consider myself so bound? You have come into my home, insulted me by calling me names, insulted my family, and then insulted me again by offering me a bribe to give up the man I love. I will not give him up, Lady Catherine, and if that was your sole design in calling here, then it is time for this visit to end, for you shall not prevail."

"Such rudeness! Obstinate, headstrong girl! I have never encountered - "

"*Silence!*" Darcy bellowed, having emerged from the book

room with Mr. Bennet after hearing raised voices in the house. "Aunt! Your coming here was extremely ill-judged, and you are not welcome if you are not prepared to be civil."

"Civil?! For my own nephew to speak to me this way is uncivil! Under the influence of this Jezebel, this common trollop!"

"Enough!" Darcy was shouting now, but as the heat of his anger increased, his voice turned cold. "Aunt Catherine, you will leave now."

"I most certainly shall not."

"Yes. Yes, you will." He nodded to his host and Mr. Bennet's two menservants stepped forward. Each seized Lady Catherine by an elbow and propelled her out the front door, held open by an astonished Mrs. Hill. Stepping to her carriage, Darcy opened the door, pulled down the steps, and stood by as his aunt was placed kicking and protesting loudly onto those steps by the Longbourn staff, who stood by prepared to immobilize her again if she showed any signs of movement back toward the house.

"I shall know how to act! I shall speak to my brother! He will make you see reason!"

A few seconds later Mr. Collins came scurrying out as well, still crying out, "Cousin Elizabeth, you have been warned. There is still time to desist from this vulgar and shameless behaviour." Darcy seized him by the elbow and glared down at him. "It is for your own protection, Mr. Darcy."

"I do not wish to be protected from your cousin, Mr. Collins."

"You are under the influence of her arts and allurements. I know them well. But - "

"Be silent, Mr. Collins. I bid you goodbye." With that he marched Collins to the carriage, boosted him up the steps as if he were a toddler, then folded up the steps, slammed the carriage door, and signaled to the coachman to be off. Lady Catherine and her rector were blessedly quiet as the carriage pulled away, and with a nod of thanks to the staff, Darcy rejoined the rest of the party in the entrance hall, where they had been watching the scene with interest. He moved directly to Elizabeth, took her hand in his, and kissed it. She gave him a watery smile and led the group back to the parlour, where Jane and Georgiana hastened to comfort her, while Anne expressed shame at her mother's behaviour and Darcy added many heartfelt apologies of his own, while reflecting privately that a short year ago he would have shared many of his aunt's most repellent attitudes. Moving to where Elizabeth sat, he squeezed her hand in unspoken gratitude that she had, as the colonel said, saved him from growing into middle age with those beliefs. She smiled up at him and placed her hand over his.

***

The wedding day dawned sunny and warm. Elizabeth rose early, as was her habit, went to the window seat, and sat quietly looking out for a few minutes, memorizing the Longbourn landscape, which she knew she would seldom see in the future. Her trunks full of wedding clothes had already been sent off to Darcy House in London, and her wedding gown hung next to Jane's in the wardrobe. She padded over to look at it. It had required substantial jousting with her mother, but it was precisely to her taste, simple and lovely, with no lace at all. *My wedding day. How many times did I wonder if this day would ever come for me, and if I would be happy.* She both felt and knew herself to be deeply happy, happier than she had ever imagined being. She looked out the window again and thought of her betrothed. Was he still asleep? She doubted it. No, he was awake, just as she was, probably looking out at the same sunrise, and - she blushed - undoubtedly thinking of her, as she was of him. *This is the last morning when I will wake up with Jane, and the last morning when I will have to wonder how he is. From now on, I will be with him, and I will know.* She blushed again, thinking on her aunt Gardiner's very reassuring advice about the duties of marriage, and grateful that she and Jane had not been forced to rely on their mother as their sole source of information.

Jane was beginning to stir. Her eyes opened slowly. She saw her sister and smiled. "Is it a nice day, Lizzy?"

"Yes, Jane, it is a beautiful day. Come, get up, and let us make some beautiful memories today." Stepping to the bed, she extended a hand to her sister, and pulled her into a fierce embrace.

The End

EPILOGUE

Seven years later, Elizabeth Darcy sat on the bench her husband had placed for her in the garden at Pemberley, absently stroking her rounded belly as her son Bennet and daughter Anne played on the lawn before her. The delightful scene seemed somehow familiar, although she knew she could never have seen it before. She puzzled until finally, remembering the dream she had had after her husband's proposal, she realised that this scene was precisely the one she had envisioned during her restless nap in her bedchamber at the Hunsford parsonage.

That parsonage was under new occupation now. Mr. Collins had succumbed to a putrid fever just a year after Darcy and Elizabeth were married, without fathering an heir to Longbourn, so Mrs. Bennet's worst fears were never realised. As Collins had been the last link in the entailment, it was now broken, and Mr. Bennet was free to bequeath the estate to anyone of his choosing. He had made his choice and Mary Bennet was the future mistress of Longbourn, much to the annoyance of her mother and her younger sisters. She had immediately begun broadening her reading to include agricultural texts and botanical treatises, and had graciously tolerated her younger sisters' fits of giggling whenever she mentioned animal husbandry. The governess Darcy had brought on for them at first had been able to do only so much to reduce their silliness, but both were now married, with babies of their own, and the demands of daily life had settled them as no hours in the schoolroom ever could.

The Bingleys were due for a visit in a few days. Finding that a lady could be settled too near her family, especially if that family were Bennet, they had purchased an estate in a neighbouring county to Pemberley, an easy drive of thirty miles with their brood of four little ones. Elizabeth was especially eager to see her goddaughter, Elizabeth Marianne Bingley, who was six years old and already spending hours in her papa's library, much as her godmother had. Elizabeth Marianne had three little brothers to dote on, but loved her visits to Pemberley, where she had a girl cousin to play with, and where her father always received good suggestions for new books to purchase for his home.

Elizabeth had invited the widowed Charlotte Collins to come and live at Pemberley for as long as she wished, since she had no real desire to return to her father's house, and she had stayed for more than two years. But during the frequent visits of the new Viscount Richard Fitzwilliam to Pemberley, an attachment had developed between them, and eventually Charlotte had consented to become the future Countess of Matlock. She had already presented the viscount with an heir, and the present earl and countess were doting grandparents.

Anne de Bourgh returned to Rosings after Darcy and Elizabeth's wedding, accompanied by Darcy's solicitors, who assisted her in confirming to her mother that Anne was the heiress and mistress of all that was Rosings. She hired a new steward whose loyalties were to her, rather than to Lady Catherine, and renovated the dower house for her mother's occupancy. She also visited the Darcys frequently and enjoyed their company. Anne's health had improved with more independence, fresh air, and exercise, but she was still not interested in marriage. She privately hoped that Elizabeth Darcy would produce a second son so that he could be the eventual heir to Rosings. It would be the closest possible outcome to her mother's dearest wish.

Mr. Bennet outlived his wife by more than ten years, and while he loved all his daughters, after being widowed he found that his Darcy grandchildren and the Darcy library provided sufficient attractions for him to spend at least half of each year at Pemberley. He eventually died during one of those visits, in his seventy-eighth year, with his favourite daughter holding his hand.

***

Made in the USA
Las Vegas, NV
04 August 2021

27539667R00108